Thy Children
to Wrath

S.M. Bankman

Outskirts Press, Inc.
Denver, Colorado

Outskirts Press, Inc.
http://www.outskirtspress.com

ISBN: 978-1-4327-4958-3

Outskirts Press and the "OP" logo are trademarks belonging to Outskirts Press, Inc.

PRINTED IN THE UNITED STATES OF AMERICA

For my sister.

Chapter 1

Fumbling around the jumbled stacks of books and magazines piled haphazardly on the bedside table, I reached for the telephone, sending the alarm clock crashing to the floor. As I mumbled a groggy, slightly chagrined hello, I felt Denise's leg brush lightly against me as she snorted in protest of her interrupted sleep.

"This is a person-to-person call from the United States for Samuel Preston," an operator announced, much too pleasantly.

"This is he," I grumbled into the receiver.

"Thank you," the operator said mechanically, "Go ahead caller." I immediately recognized the voice at the other end of the crackling line as that of my sister Iris and became instantly awake. Rarely did I receive calls from the United States, especially from a member of my family.

"Sammy," Iris began, "I have bad news." A short pause followed and then, her voice wavering, she continued.

"Rick had a heart attack this morning. He was playing softball with some kids...Rand was with him. He died before the ambulance got there."

Fully lucid, I struggled upright and switched on the bedside lamp. Squinting against the sudden light, Denise looked over at me. Grasping her arm tightly, I sat dumbfounded, the telephone receiver still to my ear. Recovering slightly from the news of my brother's death, I regained a surprisingly composed voice.

"Bubbie," I said, using Iris's childhood nickname, "what time is it in the States?"

"It's about five P.M. I'm sorry it took so long to call you. We had to medicate Mother and only she knew where your phone number was written. We had to wait for her to wake up."

"That's okay, Bub," I said, "You know I haven't exactly stayed in touch with the family. Listen, let me make a few arrangements and we should be on a plane by noon today, London time. Let's see, that should put us getting into New Orleans by around three o'clock tomorrow afternoon, your time. When is the funeral?"

"Visitation is at seven o'clock P.M. at the funeral home in LaSalle," she said. "The funeral is the next day out at Camp Harvest."

"Okay," I said. "Denise and I will join all of you at the funeral home. I hope I can remember how to get there."

After a brief pause, Bubbie said, "Sammy, *please* bring the kids. We haven't seen them in so long; they don't even know their family."

Sighing deeply, I replied, "I don't know, Bub, I'll see."

"Well please seriously think about it, Sammy," she pleaded.

"Okay, okay, I *will*...think about it, that is," I said. "I love you. I'll see you tomorrow."

Hanging up the telephone, I looked over at Denise, who was frantic, having tried desperately for several minutes to get my attention. After twelve years of marriage, my wife still became frustrated with my inability to carry on two conversations at once; a skill that came easily to her but completely eluded me. Hearing only my end of the conversation, she had become quite upset, not knowing whose dying warranted such a sudden trip across the pond.

"My brother Rick had a heart attack," I said,

caressing Denise's shoulder. "He died right away. Rand was there with him."

Denise was stunned. "Oh my God," she said, resting her hand on my arm. "Are you all right?"

"I'm not sure yet," I said. "It's been a long time since I've seen Rick, and you know what my relationship with my family has been like, but I never expected something like this. I guess you never do. Let's try to get a couple hours of sleep and we'll get going early." Denise agreed and, after returning the alarm clock to its place on the bedside table, I switched off the lamp.

About five minutes later, Denise switched on her lamp and asked, "So should I make tea?"

"Yeah, go ahead," I answered, switching my lamp back on as well. "Damn, how well you know me!"

"Of course I do, honey," she said, slipping a robe over her petite frame. "Better than you know yourself."

Sipping a wonderfully strong cup of Earl Grey, I thumbed through my address book and found the number for Heathrow Airport. Before making any arrangements, I had to decide what I was going to do with our children, eight year old Josh and ten year old Adaire. "Denise," I asked, with a sigh, "should we take the kids with us?" Denise looked at me pensively.

"I think we should, Sam. Whether you like it or not, your family is theirs as well."

I knew she was right. It would be completely inappropriate, given the circumstances, to leave Josh and Adaire in London. But the thought of my children getting anywhere near my family scared the hell out of me. And there were good reasons for that fear.

About three miles south of an obscure Louisiana highway was an old wood framed house, and in that house lived the person who had nearly ruined my life. I had vowed long ago that she would never have the opportunity to inflict her madness upon my children and because Denise and I had decided to live abroad, it had been quite easy for me to honor that vow. That person was my mother and deep down I had always known the day would come when I would have to face her again. And that day was approaching much too quickly. Feeling the almost imperceptible, yet very familiar slip into melancholy, I surrendered to the feelings that I had become so adept at keeping down. The terror that had been held captive inside me for so long began to claw its way out like rancid bile rising to the surface of my thoughts. Yes, I would have to face Prescilla Preston again, goddammit, and sooner than I had ever imagined.

Swilling down the last bit of tea, I made the necessary arrangements for our flight to the U.S. and ambled sleepily into the bathroom. I fished my electric shaver, a Christmas gift from Denise, out of the cluttered vanity drawer and switched it on. Looking into the mirror at my tired reflection, I paused momentarily, regarding what I saw. Staring back at me was the clumsy, self-conscious adolescent I had once been and on his face he wore the same downcast expression that still appeared on my own face from time to time. And in my mind I was transported back through the years to a place I had tried to forget ever existed. A place of rampant insanity. A place that should have evoked feelings of security and fulfillment, but for me brought only despondency. The place was Bayou Martin, Louisiana and it had been my childhood home.

"Get that girlie necklace off your queer neck," the woman said, through clenched teeth. "No wonder everybody at school thinks you're a weirdo."

The boy had been brushing his teeth when his mother jerked the bathroom door open, the rusted doorknob punching a hole in the shoddy sheetrock as it slammed against the wall. God, I don't need this tonight, he thought as he stared at his mother's glaring reflection angled in the steamy mirror. Already school had been a torturous eight hours, and he had hoped to be spared the bullshit that usually took place during his evenings at home. Since his last sibling had left home, refuge and protection carted away along with their suitcases and boxes, he had been the sole recipient of his mother's attention, most of it raging and angry.

"Everybody's wearing them, Mama," he said, wincing at the uncontrollable stuttering whine in his voice.

"Well only queers wear 'em where I come from," his mother continued, matter-of-factly. "No wonder you're always sleeping over at that Sonnier boy's house. Is he your boyfriend?"

"No, Mama, he's my best friend, that's all. I'm not like that."

The blow came suddenly, stinging the back of his head. Saliva flew from his mouth, spattering the mirror with foamy white speckles of Pepsodent. She was standing right behind him then, her eyes wild with rage.

"Don't dispute my word," she shrieked at him. "You'd better get down on your knees and pray that God changes you. It's an abomination, you know. Queers go to hell. Your brothers sure don't wear necklaces. But you're nothing like them anyway. You can't even play basketball, or run even one lap around a track. I can't believe I have a sissy for a son. You even look like a girl -- what is that, mascara I see on those pretty lashes? I'm glad your poor Daddy isn't alive to see this."

The boy felt pain at the mention of his father. Before he had died in an accident at the steel foundry where he had worked, the boy's father had been a wellspring of safety and security for his children, his presence usually keeping most of their mother's anger at bay. She was always gentler and even sometimes kind when he was around, and the children enjoyed it, even though they knew the reprieve would be short lived.

Delivering another slightly less severe slap to the back of the boy's head, the woman stormed out of the bathroom, slamming the door in her wake. Trembling, the boy picked up a washcloth and wiped the spittle from his face and then from the mirror. Like a discarded heap of refuse, he slumped to the floor, leaning his head against the door as the inevitable torrent of tears began to stream down his cheeks. After a few moments, he brushed away the salty drops and got up from the floor. Gazing again into the mirror, he felt the burn of hatred rise inside his gut. Struggling to stifle the explosion of emotion, he began to shake violently. The boy could not stop staring at his loathsome reflection in the mirror. Self-doubt and hatred for his world clouded everything else and the boy felt as though his head was about to explode.

All at once the shudders ceased. Still firmly transfixed by his image in the mirror, the boy raised a trembling hand to his face and calmly and systematically plucked out one eyelash. Wincing slightly from the pain, he opened the medicine cabinet behind the mirror and retrieved a pair of tweezers. He plucked out another lash, and then another, his actions becoming faster, almost frantic. The boy didn't stop the violent assault on his face until his eyelids were completely devoid of lashes.

A soft touch on my shoulder startled me as I found myself again in the present, standing in front of the marbled countertop in my own bathroom, the shaver still buzzing.

"God, Sammy, where *were* you?" Denise asked, playing soft fingers through my prematurely graying hair. "I've been standing here trying to get your attention for at least five minutes."

"Oh, I'm sorry babe," I said, "my mind was just wandering. It's just that I'm really dreading this trip. Going back to that place is bad enough, even more so under these circumstances. I bet Rand is a mess. I mean, could you imagine watching your twin brother die right there in front of you? It must have been fucking terrible."

"I know, baby," Denise said, her voice soothing and comforting. "But we'll get through this. And like it or not, your brothers and sisters need you."

Turning to face my wife, I planted a soft kiss on her forehead.

"I love you Denise," I said.

"I love you too, Sam," she answered. Falling into her embrace, I allowed a small crevice to appear in the dam as I cried softly against my wife's shoulder.

A few hours later we were finally seated on the Boeing 747 that would take us to the United States. It had been over three years since I had last crossed the Atlantic, and the anticipation was beginning to erupt into full fledged excitement. But each time I thought about the reason behind our journey, a dark veil fell across the world.

As the jet's engines roared to life, my thoughts turned to the people who were waiting for me across the pond. Despite the sick feeling in the pit of my stomach, I was actually looking forward to seeing my brothers and sisters again, and I knew that Denise had been right. We would help each other work through Rick's death. It just didn't seem right, or possible, that one of *us* was dead. Things like this just didn't happen to the Preston Kids.

My mother was deeply religious, and as far as the community had known, so were her children. Gifted with beautiful voices, not a day went by that didn't find us gathered around the old spinet piano in the living room, the lilting strains of "Precious Memories," or "Sweet Hour of Prayer" flowing out of the open windows to echo through the trees in perfect harmony. We stood in the same order each time we practiced and sang: Trevor, the oldest of the siblings, was the only bass so he stood in the rear line, to the far left. To his left stood Rick and Rand, twins, both belting out a tenor that would make Pavarotti envious. Last in line was Brett, whose magnificent range allowed him to sing whatever part needed a little boost. In the front line of the group were my sisters Faye, Bubbie, and Ruth, all three easily interchanging alto and soprano. Then there was me.

The least talented of the group, I stood next to my sisters like an afterthought, thrown in at the last moment. It didn't help matters that I was the youngest, my child's voice erupting uncontrollably at various pitch and timbre. At the piano sat my sister Rene', whose prowess on the ivories was unparalleled by anyone in Bayou Martin, including Miss Edith, the old dried-up spinster woman who had been commissioned by our mother to teach us the art of the keys. By the end of every lesson, my knuckles were always red from the sting of Miss Edith's ruler as it crashed down upon them to draw my attention to one error or another. God, how I hated those after-school lessons. The cruel tick-tock of the metronome which sat atop her ancient Baldwin upright still echoes through my mind on occasion, making me shiver with dread.

Only Rene' had escaped the wrath of the wicked ruler. At the age of eighteen months, Rene' had contracted polio. Because of this infirmity, she was always treated differently by the people in our lives. Well, except for our mother. By the time the cruel fever had run its course, Rene' was left with flaccid legs, her muscles weak and barely responsive. But thanks to a strong will and the heavy steel braces she wore throughout her childhood, she was able to walk, although with a pronounced limp. Rene' was special and all of us were very protective of her.

Every Sunday the congregation of The Harvest Church of Bayou Martin was treated to a special selection chosen just for them. According to Mama, the Holy Ghost Himself directed which songs we would sing because they always correlated perfectly with the sermon the preacher had prepared for that particular day. I'm sure it was also really helpful that the church secretary usually knew what the topic of the message would be well in advance, and that she was one of my mother's close friends. Every service ended with the standard "Just As I Am," a hymn that had always held special meaning for me. "God and I love you just the way you are," Mama would say, when in one of her rare melancholic states. What she really meant was that she recognized that I was a complete failure but she would, nonetheless, dutifully discharge the basic responsibilities due me as her offspring. I often wondered why there wasn't a hymn in the book titled "God, Please Don't Kill Me, Because I Know I'm a Freak." I could have written it myself.

To the delight of our mother, the Preston family had achieved small town fame and many times we were invited as special guests to other churches and organizations. It was after one such engagement that my sister Bubbie's life took a dark and drastic turn, a departure from rationality from which she has never fully recovered. We had been invited to provide musical entertainment to a bunch of old hens at a meeting of the Order of the Eastern Star, a women's branch of the Masonic Lodge. Bubbie had been sniffling for a few days, stricken with a summer cold inflicted upon her, no doubt, by the huge attic fan that drew the damp night air into the windows of our already drafty house. The song we had selected was called "He Touched Me," and Bubbie was to sing a whole verse as a solo. During the solo, she began to sneeze uncontrollably, mucus draining in sinewy streams from her inflamed nose. Unable to continue, she abruptly stopped singing. Looking to Mama for direction, she immediately saw the glaring, anger-effused contortion of Mama's face. Suddenly Bubbie began to cry, fountains of tears erupting from her swollen eyes, flowing down her cheeks in burning streams. The room became as silent as a morgue and seconds seemed like days as we all waited to see what would happen. The quiet was subtly broken by the pattering sound of urine cascading down Bubbie's white stockings, dripping from her shiny black shoes onto the wooden floor. Flushed with embarrassment, she ran from the platform, seeking refuge in a small bathroom. Without missing a beat, Faye, blessed Faye, picked up the solo and finished the verse. You see it was important for the song to continue so that the message of it would reach people and they would Get Saved. If you didn't sing just right, in a manner that would move the heart to realize its sinfulness, then nobody would Get Saved and when you found yourself prostrate before The Great White Throne of Judgment, their blood would most certainly be on your hands. At least it would be according to Mama.

When we had finished our selections, refreshments were served and all the ladies of the Eastern Star complimented Mama on her children's talent as well as on what a great job she was doing raising nine children with no husband. Prescilla would have died to know that everyone in Bayou Martin knew that she was barely scraping by on welfare and food stamps. Mrs. Whaler, the chairwoman of the group, whose appellation quite befitted her rather large person, was especially taken with us, exclaiming that she had never heard such beautiful music, and that if there were any unbelievers in the crowd, they would surely Get Saved after hearing the message.

Mama accepted the praise graciously, looking upon us with a well practiced pride-filled face as we sat quietly in the metal folding chairs, munching on peanuts and old-people mints. Bubbie, aided by a sympathetic lady from the small audience, had removed her stockings and although still embarrassed, looked much more composed than she had. Soon it was time to leave and we filed obediently to the door, gratefully accepting the hugs and cheek-pinching we received along the way.

As we piled into our huge white 1967 Chevrolet Impala station wagon, Mama told us that we had done well, and for a fleeting moment I thought Bubbie would be spared. But I was gravely, horribly mistaken.

"Except you," she said glaring at Bubbie. "Don't you have any self-control?" she asked, her voice taking on a dangerous edge. "Don't you ever embarrass me like that again!" she said, beginning to yell. Suddenly her hand darted across the seat, grabbing a handful of Bubbie's hair. "Learn...some...self...discipline," Mama haltingly spat through clenched teeth. With each word, she shook Bubbie's head with ever-increasing vehemence, smacking it with a dull thud against the side window of the car. Petrified, the rest of us just sat there numbly, waiting for the episode to end. Fear turned to horror as the enervating sound of shattering glass exploded from the front seat. The seemingly endless silence that followed was finally broken by Bubbie's shrill scream as blood began to pour from the gash in her head, staining the white silk bow that adorned her beautiful black hair. Mama opened the driver's door and ran around to the other side of the station wagon. Jerking open the door, she pulled Bubbie out and, grabbing the bleeding girl up, half dragged, half carried her back toward the group of women standing outside the building. The rest of us quickly poured from the car, falling over one another as we took after her.

"My God, Prescilla, what happened," Mrs. Whaler cried, her huge flaps of arm fat swinging wildly as she reached for Bubbie.

"I'm not sure," Prescilla said, real tears streaming down her face. "I was about to start the car when all of the sudden I heard this loud crash. I don't think she was all the way inside the car when she pulled the door shut. And the door won't shut all the way unless it's slammed really hard."

"Leave the rest of the children here with me and take her to the hospital in my car. I'll call my sister and she can pick us up and take us to my house."

"Oh, Myrtle, thank you," Mama said, taking the offered keys. "Kids, ya'll be good for Mrs. Whaler. And pray that Bubbie will be okay." As she turned to leave, Bubbie's face came into view and the sickening image I beheld burned itself forever into my memory. Matted with blood, Bubbie's bangs were stuck to her forehead and her eyes were glassy and vacant. I would later realize that a great part of my sister had died that night, leaving us forever. Bubbie's movements were mechanical as Mama helped her to Mrs. Whaler's car. As the car screeched across the parking lot and careened onto the highway, I felt a hand lightly touch my shoulder. It belonged to Faye, and she was weeping. Shielded glances darted between all of us kids and our eyes communicated the understanding that we would not tell anyone what had really happened. I'm not sure whether it was fear of our mother that kept us mute or the embarrassment we would experience if everyone found out about that hideous side of her personality. But I will always feel as though we betrayed Bubbie that night in the worst way, keeping silent as we did. The doctor at the emergency room had to use twenty-two stitches to close the wound in her head. And the glass from the car's window was never replaced. Trevor covered the hole with plastic and duct tape. I still remember the embarrassment I experienced when riding in the car after that.

Bubbie recovered from the physical damage that had been inflicted upon her that horrible night, but her young psyche had been forever changed. Before the incident, she had been one of those bright-eyed, cheerful people who illuminated a room just by entering it. But after that night, Bubbie seldom smiled, much less laughed. Bubbie's sullen demeanor evoked rage from Mama, and she became the brunt of most of our mother's anger. And we just sat idly by and let it happen. I believe that to this very day her soul still bleeds profusely from the events of that night. Not only had Mama crushed Bubbie's head. She had crushed her spirit as well.

A sudden lurch jolted me into the present as the 747 bumped up the runway, finally smoothing out as it took to the air. Denise, gazing at me silently, took my hand into hers. She didn't question my preoccupation. She already knew where my thoughts lay, and she didn't attempt to follow me there. From behind us, I heard the stifled giggling of Josh and Adaire as they played with the buttons and gadgets attached to the seats. I looked at my children, and I thanked God that they would never experience the trauma that had been my everyday life.

Several hours and bloody-maries later, the airplane began its descent into the New Orleans International Airport, the moss-filled tops of the cypress trees that filled the swampy landscape rose to meet us as we finally touched down. In a few minutes we had retrieved our luggage and we were heading for the rental counter to pick up our car. Although the air was saturated with humidity and the heat unbearable, it was a nice departure from the dense fog and gray skies of my adopted England. Denise suggested that we stop somewhere along the way to eat. I was famished, and a quick second of the vote by Josh and Adaire ratified the decision.

Bellies full, we were finally ready to make the three hour drive to LaSalle, and to my waiting family. By the time we reached Baton Rouge, everyone but me was sleeping, their snoring irritating me to no end. Surfing through the radio stations, I found a Cajun music program and turned the volume up to drown out the annoying noises. As we crossed the Atchafalaya Swamp Bridge, a nineteen-mile long span across some of the wildest swamplands in Louisiana, I cracked the window and lit a cigarette.

The aroma that met my nose was invigorating as the scent of wild honeysuckle invaded the car. The landscape was lush with greenery and the dogwood and Cape Jasmine were in full bloom. In some other life I would have enjoyed the lush beauty of my native home. But all of those familiar sights and smells were tainted by misery. Some of the misery was my own, some of it my siblings, and all of it Prescilla Preston's. I was dreading the reunion that would take place in less than three hours and was tempted to haul my ass back to the airport and fly home to England, back to the life *I* had created for myself, for my wife and for my children; a life that had remained untouched by the hatred and irrational violence of an insane woman.

The demons were really flying about now as I questioned just why in the hell I had come here. But etched into my mind was the image of my brother Rand, kneeling over the body of his twin, holding him as life slipped away. They needed me, I told myself. And I needed them just as badly. At that moment, I had no idea just how much I would need my brothers and sisters over the next few weeks. Rick's death was to become an unexpected catalyst that would irreversibly change every aspect of our lives.

Chapter 2

There were dozens of automobiles parked near the small funeral home in LaSalle. They lined both sides of the street and I had to park two blocks away, in front of Bill's Dollar Store. I was amazed to see that Bill's looked exactly as it had when I was a child. The same sign, although a bit weathered, still adorned the tall rusted pole that stood in front of the building. I had always loved going to the Dollar Store. The place had a distinct smell that I've always associated with newness. As we neared the front porch of the red brick building, someone was running toward me across the small lawn.

"Sammy," the person yelled, and I recognized my brother Brett. "We've been on pins and needles waiting for you to get here." I embraced my brother and was not surprised when the tears came. After hugs were exchanged between Denise, my children, and Brett, we walked up the steps and into the funeral home. The throng of people crammed into the small lobby parted as we made our way through a barrage of hellos and I'm-so-sorrys, finally reaching the rest of the family. Overwhelming emotions rendering all of us unable to speak, my siblings and I gathered into one mass embrace, unabashedly allowing the tears to flow. After a few moments, Rand spoke up.

"Do you want to see him?" he asked, motioning toward the gray casket that stood starkly against the tacky navy blue velvet curtains of the visitation room.

"Yes, but please come with me," I stammered, suddenly unsure of myself.

As I approached the casket, it occurred to me just how alive the dead appear after the mortician has worked his magic. Rick looked just as he had the last time I had seen him. The corners of his eyes were smiling and I half expected them to open. Resting my hand upon his, I recoiled slightly from the icy skin and the illusion was broken. Rick was really dead. There was no life in him, and yet it remained so intensely unbelievable. I tried to tell myself that Rick was in Heaven. That when he had Got Saved, it was real and he was with Jesus and God and everyone else who Got Saved and they were eating and singing and having a grand old time. But staring at his lifeless body, I really didn't know where his soul had gone, if indeed souls were real things. And I took secret delight in the knowledge that Prescilla would have labeled me a heretic for even considering such blasphemy. And I was infuriated that even at that moment, as I stood beside my dead brother, she was still invading my thoughts.

I lingered a few moments longer at the side of the casket and, reaching blindly for someone's, *anyone's* warm hand, found Bubbie's. Holding a handkerchief to my eyes, I let her lead me out of the visitation room and into the much too bright funeral home coffee lounge. I have always found it a bit disturbing that right across the wall from death, people can be found gorging themselves on tuna and chicken salad sandwiches, and chugging down coffee and soda as though they are at a Fourth of July picnic.

Suddenly realizing that I had been totally unaware of Denise and the kids since arriving at the funeral home, I asked Bubbie where they had gone. She told me that they were in the lobby and that

Denise's parents had arrived to pay their respects. Denise, ever vigilant of my needs, had quietly led the children out while I was standing at the casket. I fixed myself a cup of coffee and slid down onto one of the hard plastic chairs that lined the wall of the lounge. One by one my brothers and sisters entered the room, rearranging the chairs into a ragged circle so that we could all see one another. After an uncomfortable moment of silence, Brett spoke up.

"So are you still writing for that magazine, Sam," he asked, trying to sound upbeat.

"Well, sort of," I answered. "I'm the editor now."

"That's great, Sammy," another voice piped up. It belonged to Faye. "We really have missed you, brother," she said.

"I missed you too," I said, looking around at each of them. "Please forgive me for staying away for so long. I'm sorry it took, you know, *this* to get me here. But you know why..."

"Yes, we know," Rand said, softly cutting me off. "But let's talk about that later. I don't think now is a good time." Several muttered agreements resounded throughout the group.

The door opened as Denise, Josh, and Adaire came into the room. Immediately my sisters were all over them, kissing and hugging the embarrassed children. Soon everyone was engaged in various conversations, catching up on news and whatnot. We talked about Rick, remembering things about him and times we had spent with him, and the fact that he had never married. I was surprised at Rand's composure but shouldn't have been. Rick and Rand both had always been pragmatic types. Rand was taking everything in stride and seemed to be coping well. Rand's grief would surface in private, when he might one day decide to call Rick for an impromptu fishing trip and realize he wasn't there anymore. Or when he would drag out the horseshoes for a quick match at a family get-together and wouldn't have Rick there as his partner.

Some of us came and went to the visitation room, accompanying various friends and extended family, following the unspoken protocol of funeral home behavior until finally it was time for the place to close its doors for the evening. As we stood outside preparing to depart, the inevitable questions came.

"Where's Mama?" I asked. "And how is she?"

"She was here earlier," Rene' answered. "But she became extremely tired and had to leave. She said to tell you to please come stay with her while you're here."

"I guess I will," I said, not overly enthused at the prospect. "I'll see ya'll tomorrow at the funeral." After several good-byes, everyone departed. Denise had mercifully offered to drive and I dozed during the short drive from LaSalle to Bayou Martin. I awoke just as the car jounced across the first pothole in the driveway which led to the house. Thankfully, I was too tired to think about the meeting that would soon take place and only wanted sleep. A scribbled note was taped to the back door of the house:

"Sammy and Denise,

I'm sorry I'm not up to meet you, but I just couldn't go anymore today. Put the kids in your old room and you two can sleep wherever you'd like. See you in the morning."

The tone of the message was completely unlike its author's personality. Maybe she had mellowed over the years, I thought. Maybe, just maybe there was an inkling of a chance she had changed.

Unloading only what we absolutely needed for the night, we were soon in bed, sleep coming quickly. The kids were tucked away in my old bedroom, just as Mama had directed. As I slipped away from consciousness and into a welcome slumber, I searched out Denise's hand. Enjoying the security of my wife's soft touch, I was soon fast asleep.

The aroma of coffee and fried bacon teased my nose as I awoke. A unique combination, it had always been the smell of Saturday morning when I was child. Sensing the empty space next to me, I sat up and looked around for Denise. Wearing her robe, she entered the bedroom, hair glistening, a hint of apple shampoo wafting through the air. She smiled when she noticed I was awake.

"Well, good morning," she said, bending down to give me a kiss. "The kids are already up. They're having breakfast with their Grandma."

"What kind of mood is she in," I asked, feeling the familiar weight of apprehension pressing against my chest.

"Actually," Denise began, "she's been very friendly. She started to cry when Josh and Adaire met her in the kitchen. Why don't you go have some coffee with them? There's not a lot of time until we have to leave for the funeral."

I got up from the bed and, throwing on my robe, headed down the hallway into the kitchen. The sight of my mother startled me. She had aged quite rapidly since the last time I had seen her. Her face was etched with creases and lines and her hair had become starkly white. A slight bow had appeared in her back and her shoulders drooped forward, making it appear as though she had shrunk. She was sitting in her usual place at the end of the table, the newspaper opened to the daily crossword.

"Hello Mama," I said, as I poured my coffee.

"Well don't I get a hug?" she asked, appearing truly hurt. Bending down, I loosely placed my arms around her neck and executed the most perfunctory of hugs.

"I'm glad you're here, son," she said, beginning to cry.

"This is so hard for me. I've always prayed that I would never have to see one of my children go before me." Perhaps because of my extreme cynicism concerning my mother or perhaps because of my experiences with her, I perceived her every word as measured and contrived.

I wanted so badly to believe that at least a small part of what she was saying was the truth. Maybe she really did love her children. Maybe I had imagined her being worse than she really was. No, I thought to myself, I'm not going to play that fucking game with myself and set myself up for certain disappointment. Nonetheless, I could not help but offer this miserable woman the basic courtesies that humanity demands. Taking a seat at the table, I took her hand into mine.

"I'll stay for a while, Mama," I said. "You're right, it has been too long. Besides, my kids will never forgive me if I don't let them spend some time here.

"Grandma said there's a big rope swing in the back yard," Adair chimed in.

"There sure is," I said. "It's been there since I was your age. I spent hours on that swing."

"Can we go see it?" Josh asked.

"No, son, we have to go the funeral today," I answered.

"Oh, yeah," he said solemnly. "For Uncle Ricky."

"Would you like to ride with us?" I asked, directing the question to my mother.

"That would be great," she answered. "I don't drive all that much anymore. Kind of scares me." I was sure it scared everyone else, too.

"Well I'm going to get dressed," I said, sliding the chair back away from the table. "Come on kids, time to get ready."

"Sammy," my mother said, as I walked out of the kitchen.

"Ma'am?" I answered.

"Thank you," she said. I smiled briefly and went to get dressed. In a short while we were on our way to the small gray cinderblock chapel that stood next to the cemetery at Camp Harvest. Prescilla rode quietly, staring out of the window, the silence uncomfortable. Suddenly, she spoke, and the Prescilla of my youth was once again in my presence. Apparently she had decided that the initial pleasantries were finished and it was okay for her to tear into me.

"You really should be ashamed, you know," she said, glaring at me from the passenger's seat. "You have to wait for someone to die to come see your family. You probably haven't spoken to Rick in years. Its no surprise you aren't even upset." I started to retort and then bit my lip. Even as an old woman, she knew what buttons to push, and damn it, I wasn't going to be sucked into a confrontation.

"Well?" she said, continuing to stare at me.

"Well, what, Mama?" I asked, angry at myself for even acknowledging her comments. "What's wrong, am I not behaving in your prescribed manner? What the hell do you want, to see me flailing around in an emotional stupor?"

"Don't curse in front of me, boy," she said, familiar coarseness in her voice. "I see you're still rebellious. Do you even take your children to church? They probably don't even know who God is. But that's what happens when you marry a..."

Thoroughly pissed off by that point, I cut her off.

"That's enough, Mama," I almost yelled. "This isn't the time." Thankfully she chose to keep her mouth shut, avoiding further argument. I had involuntarily finished her sentence in my mind -- she had been about to refer to my wife as a pagan Catholic. She had always loved that phrase, oblivious to the oxymoron. A few moments later, she commented on how pretty the magnolia blooms were that dotted the countryside. It had always amazed me how quickly her demeanor could change. It was as though her harsh words had never been spoken. Nonetheless, I was thankful that she had softened, if only for a moment. I gazed into the rearview mirror and was relieved to see that both Josh and Adair were listening to their portable compact disc players and had been oblivious to the exchange between my mother and me. Denise, on the other hand, had heard every word and a troubled look creased her brow. I winked at her in the mirror and this seemed to help a little. But Denise knew at that point that Prescilla was still the same old bitch she had always been.

As we drove between the huge oak trees that lined the road leading onto the grounds of Camp Harvest, I remembered the wonderful times I had spent and the camp as a child. Several of the area churches had formed the camp back in the 1940s, as a means to spread the gospel message and Save as many children as possible. Rick had been very active in his church and at the camp. This fact made it even more difficult to believe that Rick's life had ended at the young age of forty-five. Rick had been one of those rare people who lived their faith with zeal but with a marked absence of the arrogance and prejudices that usually accompany the deeply religious. It was because of such contradictions that my own faith had become nearly nonexistent since I had left home. I had a hard time understanding the desire some had to worship such a hateful God. And hateful was the only way to describe most of the regulars at the Harvest Church of Bayou Martin, to include my mother.

At a very early age, I had been introduced to a vengeful God who was just waiting to strike me down for one sin or another. I remember the night that the Dugas's house had burned to the ground. The Dugas family lived about three miles down the road from us and we went to school and church with them. According to Prescilla Preston, God had a reason for everything and she knew exactly what all of those reasons were. The Dugas's were getting just what they deserved.

A couple of years before the tragic fire, , the Dugas's youngest daughter, Kaye, had been seen leaving the parking lot of Slim's Place, a night club in the nearby town of LaSalle, where all the pagan Catholics went to get drunk and have sex. When the *preacher-du-jour* at the Harvest Church found out about it, he paid a special visit to the Dugas's home. He informed Mrs. Mary Dugas that Kaye needed to "get right with the Lord" and confess before the congregation what she had done. Well this just didn't sit right with Mrs. Dugas and she told the preacher that she wouldn't hear of it. In no uncertain terms, the preacher informed Mrs. Dugas that if she didn't comply they would no longer be welcome at the Harvest Church of Bayou Martin.

The following Sunday the Dugas's usual pew was vacant. So of course, the "prayer chain" had to be activated to pray for the family's wayward souls. Prayer chain -- *gossip* chain was a more accurate description. No one's lives were safe from the prayer chain. It was the lifeline of the church. Every old biddy in the church would immediately know, for example, that a strange vehicle could be seen parked every Thursday in Peggy Colombe's driveway. And also they would know that Peggy's husband left every Wednesday night for a week-long stint of work with an offshore oil company. "I just thought you needed to know," the initiator of the chain would say, "so you can pray for her." It didn't matter that Peggy Colombe's husband beat the shit out of her on a regular basis. Or that for over a year he had been carrying on an affair with Chastity Bergeron who worked at the post office.

Nope, if you didn't belong to the inner circle of the Harvest Church of Bayou Martin you didn't have a chance in hell of not going straight to the wretched place to burn there forever and ever. And according to Prescilla Preston, such was the case with the Dugas family. After being spurned by the church, the Dugas's had accepted the kind invitation of Mrs. Thigpen, the local Avon lady, to visit mass at St. Martin de Tours Catholic Church in LaSalle. A few weeks later, every phone in Bayou Martin was ringing off its hook as the gossip chain did its thing. Apparently the preacher's wife was coming out of the Rexall Drugstore in LaSalle one day and saw Mary Dugas's Town Car parked in the front. And hanging from the rear-view, in plain sight for everyone to see, was a brand new rosary! "Can you believe it?" the preacher's wife had said to the first link in the gossip chain. "Mary Dugas worshipping their Mary-god!"

So even though the fire chief had stated that a leaky propane gas line had been the culprit, Mama knew better. The house had burned, no doubt, because of the family's turning away from the true church to cling to the Great Whore of Babylon and they were only getting a sample of what awaited them when they burned in the Lake of Fire forever. What sticks in my mind about the whole thing is that in their younger days, Mama and Mary Dugas had been best friends. No, I was finished with religion and with God, so I had thought. It would be some time before I uttered the first prayer.

The funeral I attended that day at Camp Harvest was one of the saddest events in my life. Emotions flowed freely as we listened to the eulogy. Mama was stoned-faced through the entire service. Not a single tear. I'd like to believe it was the mega dose of valium that maintained her stoic composure. But deep down inside I believe that she simply felt no grief. As we filed past the casket that held my brother's body and exited through the side door of the chapel, it seemed as though the world was emptier than it had been when I had entered the chapel. The sky was not quite as blue; the trees not as green; and the trivialities of life suddenly became extremely important.

After the funeral all of the Preston kids converged at our childhood home, seeking and finding solace in each other's company. Sensing our need to be alone, Denise suggested to the other spouses that everyone gather up their kids and go down to the gazebo near the bayou for coffee and cookies. Feeling a twinge of guilt, I watched as my children bounded across the lawn with their cousins whom they hardly knew. Despite the circumstances, I was happy to see them enjoying themselves.

Mama sat in complete silence in her recliner by the window, a cat draped lazily across her lap. My brothers, sisters, and I shared "remember when" stories about our childhood and we were really beginning to enjoy being together. Obvious to all of us, the special closeness we had always held for one another was still there even after all the years of separation. In an abrupt flurry of fur, Mama unexpectedly sprung up from her chair, sending the startled tabby tumbling unceremoniously to the floor.

"I can't take it, I can't take it," Prescilla screamed, slumping to the floor in a pitiful heap. Immediately we all hopped up from our seats and my sisters Faye and Bubbie were at her side helping her up and leading her out of the den. She was still babbling incoherently as they helped her into her bed and popped a couple of the tiny yellow valium into her mouth. I hastily sat back down on the couch, cradling my face in my hands. Trevor, Rand and Brett, who had never easily dealt with adverse situations, had made a quick exit onto the patio, leaving only Rene' and Ruth with me in the den. Ruth sat down next to me and draped her arm across my shoulders. Fearing that I was overcome with emotion, she asked if I was all right. I wasn't crying, however. I was laughing. And this agitated Ruth to a very high degree. As she quickly pulled her arm away from me and stood up, Faye and Bubbie came back into the room.

"Sam, what in the hell is the matter with you?" Ruth asked, placing her hands on her hips in true pissed-off-woman fashion.

"What's going on now?" Faye asked, sighing as she plopped down into a chair.

"Did ya'll see that shit?" I asked, my lips curling into a sardonic smile. "Somebody give her an Oscar. That was the best fucking performance I've seen all year!"

"What are you talking about, Sammy?" Faye asked.

"Oh come on," I said. "It's obvious. She never could stand it that we were so close and it's killing her that we're all here together. She feels threatened, Faye, and that little display was just the right thing she needed to place everyone's focus back on her." The door opened and my three brothers came back into the den.

"How's Mama," Trevor asked, sitting next to me on the couch.

"I'm sure she's sailing with Prince Valium by now," I said, sarcastically.

"Really, Sammy, you're being an ass," Ruth said. "She just lost a son."

"Oh please," I said, a slight edge to my voice. "She didn't even like him."

"God, Sam, how can you say that. He was her son," Bubbie said.

"She doesn't like any of us, Bubbie," I said, cutting her off. "I don't think she ever has."

"How can you act this way right now?" Rene' interjected. "Maybe you don't feel any grief right now, but *we* do. *We* haven't been hiding in England for the past eight years like some people I know."

"I feel just as much fucking grief as anyone else here," I half yelled, jumping to my feet. "And what the hell do you know about guilt? You think it's been easy being away from all of you? But you know goddamn well why I've stayed away. You all may have forgotten what it was like here, but I sure as hell haven't and I never will." I was fuming by then, and my angry outburst had cast a hush across the room. Faye was first to break the silence.

"Sammy, please stop cursing and using the Lord's name in vain," she said. "There's really no need for all this."

"I agree," Rene' added.

"Oh, okay," I snapped back angrily. "I won't say fuck, we'll pretend our mother isn't insane, and we'll just all pretend that Rick isn't really six feet under at the Camp Harvest fucking cemetery." Immediately I regretted the outburst. Considering just how big an asshole I really was, I watched the tears streaming down my sisters' faces.

"Oh, God, I'm so sorry," I said, collapsing on the couch. "Faye, Rene', you're absolutely right. I'm just so mired in my own bullshi-, I mean crap, that I'm almost blind to everyone else's needs."

"Why don't we all get some rest," Rand interjected, his level head prevailing as usual. "This has been a horrible day. I think we all need to take some time to get ourselves on more even keel."

"That's a good idea, Rand," Brett said. "Ya'll remember the park on the river near my house? If everyone can get approval from their better halves, why don't we meet out there on Saturday? Bring your kids. It would be nice to spend some time together before everyone goes their separate ways."

Trevor spoke up. "Is anyone staying here with Mama? She really shouldn't be alone right now."

"Denise and I will be here," I said. "But I would appreciate it if one of you would stay with me. Denise really wants to visit her parents while we're here. It's been a few months since their last visit to London."

"I'll stay," Bubbie said. Everyone in the room suddenly turned in unison and looked at her in obvious disbelief. "I have a few days of vacation. I really don't mind."

I am sure that at that moment, each of us was thinking the same thing. Of all of us, Bubbie was the last one who should have any desire at all to stay with Mama. But we all kept our reservations to ourselves. I, for one, was extremely grateful for her offer.

Standing in the driveway, batting away the squadrons of mosquitoes that were skillfully dive-bombing every patch of exposed skin, I waved good-bye to my brothers and sisters, promising them I would see them again on Saturday. Scolding and fussing, Denise appeared at the crest of the hill behind the house, Josh and Adaire in tow. The children's hair was matted with mud, their clothes were soaked, and they were absolutely delighted at their condition. The bayou that snaked its way through the swamp behind my childhood home had always been too strong a temptation to resist for any child, and I wasn't surprised that they had somehow "fallen in." Twisting the handle on the outdoor water faucet, Denise made kids strip off their soiled clothing. Rising from her neck to her ears, a slight flush spread across Adaire's face as she slipped the mucky sundress over her head. Both children began to giggle as the cold water from the hose splashed across their pale bodies.

An activity usually reserved for country children, stripping down to their undies outside was a new experience for the two city dwellers and they were enjoying it immensely.

"Josh, stop looking!" Adaire squealed, covering the important parts with her hands. Handing each of them a towel, Bubbie laughed at their antics. Bubbie had an unusually light-hearted air about her that night. She was behaving as though she had suddenly become unencumbered of some heavy burden and for a fraction of an instant, I found her demeanor a bit strange, considering her usual sullenness.

Denise and the kids having gone inside for the evening, I took advantage of the opportunity to be completely alone and wandered down to the gazebo by the bayou. The rising moon was just beginning to peek through the tops of the tall pines and cypress of the swamp and the shadows cast by the pale light were strange and mysterious and wonderful. As I sat down on the wooden bench inside the gazebo, a Whip-Poor-Will sounded its hello to the night and a hoot owl answered in eerie response.

Filching a cigarette from my shirt pocket, I considered everything that had transpired over the previous few days. Never had I imagined that I would ever sit there again, at the bayou's edge listening to the frogs, crickets, and other sounds that made up the symphony of a Louisiana night. I had never planned to see that place again, except, maybe, to take care of the final disposition of my mother's property. It just wasn't fair, I thought, watching the ghostly swirls of smoke dissipate into the humid air as I exhaled. That Rick, with all the goodness he had to offer this wretched world, should be snuffed out in his prime while mean-spirited, hateful people with black souls lived to be a fucking hundred years old seemed to me the ultimate injustice. I should have attended her funeral that day, not Rick's.

Stubbing the cigarette out on the underside of the bench, I got up and stepped down from the gazebo onto the soft grass. As I climbed the gentle slope that led up from the bayou to the house, my attention was drawn to the windows that looked out onto the back yard from my old bedroom. Through the bamboo shade that hung over the window, Denise's silhouette was starkly outlined. I watched as she slipped off her robe and brushed her hair, her perfectly rounded breasts swaying gently with the motion of her arms. I still couldn't believe that I had her. And I wondered if she knew that she was my salvation from the madness that had surrounded me throughout my life. It frightened me to think of living without her.

I had met Denise when I was only sixteen years old. A newcomer to LaSalle High, I had moved from the school in Bayou Martin because Mama wanted me to be in the marching band and the tiny school I had attended since kindergarten had no music program whatsoever. I didn't want to switch schools. All of my friends were in Bayou Martin, but of course I had no say-so in the matter. Living her life vicariously through me, as she always had, Mama envisioned grand parades and concerts, with her son expertly leading the band. I would be drum major of the band, she had said, because most of the students in LaSalle were just stupid coonasses (a sometimes derogatory term used to describe Louisianans of Cajun French heritage) and my abilities would far surpass theirs.

In fact, I didn't have the first desire to be in the band or to hold the be-all-end-all post of drum major. Male drum majors were without exception harassed endlessly by the other boys in the school and I didn't need another situation to make my school life even more miserable. I had always been called "faggot" and "queer" at school and flitting around in a lacy white suit and fancy white gloves would only lend a sort of confirmation to the accusations. Of course, I could share none of my reservations with my mother. She would have taken it as rebellion against her all encompassing authority and made life even more miserable. So I just kept my thoughts to myself.

The first time I saw Denise, she was standing on a white plywood podium at the edge of the band's practice field, her elegant hands inscribing upon the air a perfect 3/4 time. It was Monday of the second week of the LaSalle High School summer band camp, and I arrived there just as they were finishing up for the day. I had to meet the band director and let him know I would be a new member, planning to begin practice the following day. Denise was the newly appointed drum major at that time and was quite good at it, directing the gangly gaggle of woodwind and brass musicians through every crescendo and every staccato. She was wearing white cotton shorts and through them I could make out the curves of her young body. At sixteen, my hormones were constantly working overtime and I felt a familiar stirring between my legs as I took in her beauty. Just then, I was startled by a gruff yell in my ear.

"Forget it, bud," my new friend Richard said. "You'll never get her attention. Denise is a goody-two-shoes. She doesn't even drink."

"Yeah, well, we'll just see," I said, determination in my voice. "She's beautiful, Richard."

"No way," Richard said, with surety. "She doesn't put out."

"That's not what I meant, dickhead," I said, punching Richard playfully in the arm. "I want to *know* her."

"Go ahead, don't listen to me, asshole," he replied, "you're just setting yourself up for a hellacious fall."

The band director barked a garbled "dismissed" through his megaphone and the tired marchers hurried off the field toward the band room doors. As Denise climbed down from the podium, I took a deep breath and approached her.

"Hey," I said, nonchalantly. "My name is Sam. I just moved here."

"I'm Denise," she answered, eyeing me warily.

"Uhm, I was thinking that maybe after band practice we could get a coke or something."

"I really have to go home," she said, nervously. "I have homework and my Mom likes for me to go straight home after practice."

"Oh, okay," I said, trying to hide my disappointment. "Maybe some other time."

"Yeah, maybe," she answered and walked toward the band room.

Totally embarrassed by the rejection, I walked slowly toward the band director, who was still standing near the field, making notations on a pad. I introduced myself to him and after he lectured me with the standard motivational rhetoric, I made my way to the school's graveled parking lot. As I was about to climb into the seat of the old pickup truck left to me by Brett when he moved away, I noticed Denise, on the opposite end of the parking lot, putting a key into the door of an old Ford Pinto. My heart pounding, I quickly put the key into the ignition and fired up the old truck. I drove across the parking lot and stopped right next to her. Rolling down the window, I smiled and Denise smiled nervously back at me.

"Are you coming to practice tomorrow?" she asked.

"Yeah," I said, overwhelmed once again by the girl's subtle beauty. "I'm going to play tuba."

"Cool," she said, engaging the Pinto's starter. "Tell you what, after practice I'll take you up on that coke." I couldn't believe her words and my excitement must have been evident, for a broad smile spread across her face.

"Great!" I almost yelled. "See you tomorrow." Navigating the winding back road that ran between Bayou Martin and LaSalle, the radio blaring and the wind blowing through my hair, I was the king of the world. Maybe, I thought to myself, the long dry season of loneliness in which I had been lost for the better part of my life was about to come to an end. I hardly noticed my mother that night, too engrossed in my own thoughts to pay any attention to her words.

Supper passed in merciful silence and I was soon in my bed. Lying there listening to the rattle and hum of the ancient attic fan that ventilated the house, I stared at the ceiling, dimly lit by the moonlight seeping in through the bamboo shade. Still excited about my date with Denise, it was hours before I finally fell asleep.

The next morning I got up early, feeling energetic and excited. Mama commented that she was happy to see me so eager to start band practice. But as usual she warned against setting myself up for the disappointment that would surely come should I "screw it all up."

Like a resilient suit of mail, the anticipation of spending time with Denise hung upon me, deflecting any arrows my mother could launch. Driving down the road (much to fast), I turned the radio up as loud as it would go, my head nodding involuntarily to the driving beat of the heavy metal music blaring from the cheap speakers. I spent the morning sitting in the band room learning the basic fingerings of the tuba and, having already learned to read music while taking piano lessons, soon deciphered which valves to depress to achieve the written notes on the page. The band director was amazed that I had picked it up so quickly. By the afternoon, he had me on the field learning the formations that would make up the band's half-time performance for the opening game of football season. Time was passing quickly and I realized that I was actually enjoying myself. Maybe being in the band would be all right after all, I thought. Besides, being there meant that I would see Denise every day, and I would have endured all of the fires of hell just to glimpse her from afar.

Soon practice was finished and the instruments put away in their little wooden cubicles in the band room. I hurried from the building. Trying my best to look suave, I leaned against the door of my truck and lit a cigarette. I saw Denise walking toward me across the parking lot and glanced quickly into the truck's side mirror, trying to push my ruffled hair into place. Denise finally reached me and I opened the door and offered my hand to help her into the truck.

An exhilaration I had never before experienced coursed through me as she placed her soft hand into mine. In an uncomfortable silence, we drove to the Dairy Queen down the street from the school. Once inside, I finally spoke up.

"You do a good job as drum major," I said, sipping on my coke. "I think its cool." My words sounded silly as they leapt from my mouth. I had planned out exactly what I would say to her, but I became retarded as I sat there in front of her.

"Thank you," Denise said. "You picked up on the tuba fast."

"Yeah, I guess," I answered. "So what classes do you have this year?"

Soon, with the ice officially broken, we were chatting away as if we had known each other for years. We covered every subject that two teenagers could have in common -- music, parents, school -- and it became apparent that we were enjoying each others' company. In the following days we fastidiously kept our date at the Dairy Queen. One hot afternoon we passed up our usual meeting place and drove down a rough dirt road that led to a beautiful sandbar nestled in a bend of the Quelquechou River. After kicking off our shoes, we walked along the edge of the sandbar, the icy cold water refreshing and crisp on our bare feet. Pausing for a moment, I gazed across the river at the rows of cypress trees that lined the narrow stream. It was then that I felt Denise's hand slip into mine.

Turning to face her, I planted a soft kiss on her cheek first and then her lips. That was the first time I had attempted any kind of intimate contact with Denise (or any girl for that matter) and my movements were nervous and clumsy. But the tension that had been subtly building between us for several weeks was finally broken. Once again pressing my lips against hers, I encircled her waist with my arms, pulling her tightly against me. I began to shake as I felt her firm breasts against my chest, her nipples protruding ever so slightly through her cotton tee shirt. Our tongues probing and searching in passionate kisses, we moved as one down onto the hot sand. With the insistence and ferocity of young lovers charting undiscovered realms of passion, she pressed her body harder and harder into my loins, my virgin stiffness pushing painfully against my jeans. Completely relinquishing ourselves to our desires, we quickly shed our clothes, bare skin touching, sending alien, fiery sensations up and down my body.

With raw, inexperienced innocence, we helped each other guide everything into the right place. Pushing slowly into her, I planted soft kisses on her neck and breasts, further excited by the rise and fall of her chest as her breathing became more rapid. Raising her hips to meet my gentle thrusts, she lightly ran her fingers through my hair, creating even more sensations. We gave ourselves to one another completely that day at the river, spiritually as well as physically. And although it did not take very long for our lovemaking to meet its peak, we both lay there on the soft sand, totally spent.

During the remaining two years of high school, Denise and I remained together save for a few temporary separations, results of the unpredictable emotional upheavals common to those in their teens. It was always understood by both of us that we were meant to be together. The fact was never questioned. So it was no surprise to anyone when I asked her to marry me after my first year in the U.S. Army. Anyone that is, except for Prescilla Preston. I had managed, miraculously, to keep my relationship with Denise hidden from my mother.

I adamantly refused to afford Mama an opportunity to mar the beauty I shared with my Denise. When I went home for a thirty day leave, the news of my upcoming marriage took Mama by complete surprise. A week after arriving home, Denise and I were married during a small ceremony in her parent's home. Surprisingly enough, Prescilla was pleasant at the ceremony, even civil to the handful of guests. I think she was so magnanimous because she was relieved that I hadn't turned out to be "a queer abomination." Whatever the case, I hadn't really cared one way or the other what her demeanor was like.

Denise and I traveled Europe together over the following three years, falling in love with England, the city of London in particular. My date of separation from the military quickly arrived and the decision to remain in Europe was an easy one to make. Drawing upon my experience as a field journalist in the Army, I applied for a job that involved writing a monthly column for a London magazine. The editor of the magazine had recognized a growing potential for gaining new readers in the increasing number of Americans living and working in England. The enormous and positive response to *Briterrica*, the name of the monthly feature, led the owner to develop it into a completely separate magazine.

I was elated when he asked me to edit the new creation. Sales skyrocketed, attracting the attention of an abundance of advertisers and the following months found us quite comfortable, financially. Taking advantage of programs offered by the military, Denise had obtained a master's degree in elementary education. Shortly after I separated from the Army and we moved to London, Denise took a job teaching English at a private London school, taking only enough time off to have Josh and Adair. We were happy in the life we had created for ourselves. Denise's parents, both retired from their respective careers, flew to London quite often to visit. Separated by time and distance from my sordid past, I had thought myself rid of the demons that had plagued me as a child.

But there I found myself, standing in the back yard of my mother's house, older, wiser, but still tethered to a terrible past from which I couldn't seem to free myself. Long forgotten memories, newly recalled, reached greedily across the expanses of time, drawing me again into their relentless claws. Swatting mosquitoes, I continued toward the back door of the house, never taking my eyes off of the window that displayed my wife's sensuous silhouette.

Eerily quiet when I entered it, the house seemed to recognize me, to welcome me with an "I-told-you-so" audible in the sighs and creaks of its wood frame. Bubbie was sleeping on the sofa bed in the den so I closed the door silently behind me and went down the hall to my room and my wife. Emotionally and mentally exhausted, I lay down next to Denise, resting in the secure and familiar feel of her soft hair nestled against my chest. Good night, Rick, I thought to myself. Tell God we really need Him down here.

Chapter 3

The next several days passed by quietly. Mama remained happily lost in a drug-induced stupor most of the time, which was fine with me. She spent the better part of her day resting in her chair by the window or lying in her bed staring up at the ceiling. Occasionally she was lucid enough to engage in some conversation, but for the most part remained aloof. This created a great opportunity for me to spend time catching up on family news with Bubbie, and to introduce my children to those secret joys unique to my native home. I was actually beginning to enjoy my stay in Bayou Martin when my entire world plunged headlong into a tailspin for the second time in as many weeks.

On a bright sunlit morning, I sat on the patio sipping coffee, mesmerized by two hummingbirds sipping sugar water from one of those cheap plastic feeders made to look like flowers. Denise and the children had left the day before to spend a couple of days at her parents' home, promising to rejoin me for the visit at the park near Brett's house. Enjoying the solitude, I was about to peruse the morning newspaper when the sliding glass door which led onto the patio opened and Bubbie stepped out.

With the emotional flatness of a news anchor, Bubbie made an announcement:

"Mama's dead," she said, then turned slowly and walked back nonchalantly into the house. All I could do was sit and stare stupidly at the hummingbirds flitting around the feeder. Wishing I could instantly transport myself to another planet, I laid the newspaper down on the patio table and went into the house. With calmness that sent the whole situation headlong into the surreal, Bubbie stood at the kitchen counter stirring a pink packet of sugar substitute into a fresh cup of coffee. I felt nothing. No panic, no grief, no emotion at all. With the sort of detachment usually observed in doctors, torturers and homicide detectives, I walked into Prescilla's bedroom, stopping involuntarily a few paces away from the old canopy bed in which she lay. The emotion came suddenly, unexpectedly as I looked upon her lifeless face. In earlier years, I had thought much about this day, even looked forward to it. But as I stood there in the quiet room, the slight breeze from the ceiling fan lightly ruffling my hair, the sobs so shook me that I could only sit down on the floor until the wave subsided. I would later realize that I had not cried that morning for what my mother had been. No, I had mourned what could have been. And I raged over the knowledge that it was too late for me to ever find out.

After a few moments practicality overcame emotion and I collected myself enough to consider the necessary steps that would have to be taken. First I needed to talk to Bubbie and find out what had transpired that morning. Her flat demeanor lent even more strangeness to the situation. Drying my face and eyes with a Kleenex, I went back into the kitchen. Bubbie was sitting at the table staring fixedly into space.

"When did you discover it," I asked, taking a seat next to Bubbie.

"This morning," she answered, dryly. "I went into her room to tell her that the coffee was ready. When she didn't stir, I went over to the bed and touched her arm. It was cold, Sammy. So cold. I leaned down and put my face near hers. I couldn't feel her breath on my cheek. That was when I knew."

"Why the hell didn't you wake me up?" I asked, slight anger in my voice. Bubbie stared at me for a few strange moments and then began to speak.

"I did it, Sammy," Bubbie said, looking intently into my eyes.

"Did what?" I said, genuinely confused.

"I killed her."

"Bubbie, what the fuck is going on here?"

"After you and Denise went to bed, I went into her room, woke her up, and told her it was time to take her medicine again. It was so easy. She just opened her mouth and took all the pills with no fuss at all. She washed them down with a little water and that was that. For some reason I thought it would be, you know, a lot harder. When I first went into her room this morning she still looked alive. I thought that maybe I hadn't given her enough pills. But then she didn't wake up when I called to her. Anyway, you can call the police now. I'm ready."

Staring in disbelief as my sister explained how she had overdosed our mother, I suddenly realized that at some point I had got up from the table, and had backed up against a wall, unconsciously recoiling from this person whom I loved so much.

Then I remembered Bubbie's uncharacteristic levity a few nights before and realized that she had planned this thing. God only knows how many years she had wanted to do it, and when the opportunity had presented itself, she had grabbed onto it with both hands. Bubbie began to cry as she noticed what must have been horror contorting my face. Suddenly, the woman sitting there at the table before me did not have the face of a murderess. Instead, I saw the face of the little girl with the white bow in her hair, wearing shiny new shoes, who so many years before had suffered at the hands of our deeply disturbed mother. It was then that I walked across the kitchen and put my arms around my sister, allowing her to cry. After a few moments, she had composed herself and I knew it was time for me to figure out what to do.

"You know we really do have to call the police," I said, picking up the telephone book. "We have to tell them what happened, Bubbie."

"I know," she said. "Call them. And Sammy?"

"Yes, Bub," I answered.

"No matter what happens, it's over." The finality with which Bubbie delivered those two words chilled my blood. No matter what happened after that day, for my sister the nightmare was indeed over.

Mr. Edmund Deloux, chief detective of the Martin Parish Sheriff's Office arrived about thirty minutes after I placed the call, two deputies accompanying him. I had asked to speak to Mr. Deloux specifically and had only told him that a death had occurred and to please come. A kind man, he was familiar with my family as I had attended school with his son, Michael.

Soon after their arrival, a black Chevrolet Suburban with the words "Martin Parish Coroner" affixed to its front doors came up the driveway and pulled onto the carport behind the detective's shiny white Crown Victoria cruiser. Photos were taken, evidence gathered and none of it seemed to be really happening. With the help of the deputies, the coroner placed Prescilla's body in a black bag and wheeled it out of the house, loading it into the Suburban. Fishing through the drawers of Prescilla's dresser, I found the envelope which contained her burial policy and gave it to the coroner. He agreed to contact the funeral home as soon as the inevitable autopsy had been performed. I thanked him and watched as the black vehicle bounced down the driveway. Horrified with myself, I stifled an inappropriate giggle as I imagined the black bag that contained my mother's body flouncing around the back of the Suburban and hoped that it was strapped down.

I was surprised at how calm Bubbie remained throughout it all. She readily responded to the detective's initial questions, but when he began to realize what had taken place he advised my sister to say nothing more until she had spoken with an attorney. He read her the standard Miranda and soon she was sitting quietly in the back seat of the cruiser.

Before getting into the car, the detective turned to me and recommended that I remain available to answer any further questions and expressed his condolences. Accepting a firm handshake, I assured him that he need only pick up the phone and I would be there at a moment's notice. I walked to the rear of the car and, pressing my hand against the window glass, mouthed an "I love you" to Bubbie. As the car rolled slowly away, she turned and looked at me through the rear window. I stood in the driveway staring after her as the white car disappeared behind the baby's breath and crepe myrtle that lined the driveway.

For a few moments I stood there, looking around the yard. I noticed that the cape jasmine that grew along the side of the house were beginning to bloom, pungent white flowers opening in beautiful blossoms. How could I notice this, right now, on this day, I thought to myself. It seemed obscene to think about something as trivial as a flowering bush on the morning of my mother's death. Then I realized what had drawn my attention to the bush in the first place. It was the bush to which Mama would send us to cut our own switches when her old ones would wear out.

Turning slowly, I walked into the house, fished Mama's address book from the roll top desk in the den and sat down, the telephone in my hand. With trepidation, nauseated at the thought of doing it, I dialed Faye's number. It only took me a few minutes to relate to her what had taken place, and she reacted much the same way as I had standing in Mama's bedroom earlier that morning. After she calmed down, she agreed to make the calls necessary to inform the rest of the family of the terrible happenings. Needless to say, the Saturday barbeque would be cancelled. I was grateful to Faye for calling everyone else to let them know about what happened. I don't think I could have taken it as my brothers and sisters each heard of Mama's death, especially considering the circumstances surrounding it.

I dialed the phone once again, this time to call Denise. I didn't tell her everything then, only that something had happened and that I was on my way to meet her at her parents'.

As I hung up the phone, I was suddenly acutely aware of the silence that permeated the house. A chill penetrated to my very soul and an unnamed fear summoned goose bumps on my arms and neck. The house suddenly seemed very large and very empty, the slightest creak echoing through-out the place with orchestral resonance. I didn't even bother to lock the door as I hurried out and climbed up into Mama's truck. Wheels spinning, churning up a spray of gravel, dust and grass, I sped down the driveway, not even slowing for the massive potholes that cratered the poorly main-tained road. Screeching onto the narrow macadam pavement, I felt the familiar bristling of the tiny hairs on my neck. As a teen, I had experienced that sensation often, afraid to look in the rear view mirror for fear that something was following me, and gaining on me with every second that passed. Whatever demons were after me that day had re-linquished their chase disappointed, for I didn't slow the truck at all until I reached the highway, at which point the feeling subsided. Soon I was with

Denise and the turmoil of the morning began to slowly subside.

Later that night the Preston children, this time minus two, were once again gathered at their childhood home. We had all agreed to meet there without our families to discuss what had happened as well as what might lie before us. Denise, my rock, had the presence of mind earlier that day to suggest that I get in touch with my office staff to inform them that my stay in the United States would be indefinitely extended. It was agreed that once a week I would be available via Internet to review their work concerning the magazine and I instructed them to telephone or email with any problems that might arise.

Lighting a cigarette, I gazed around the room at my brothers and sisters. Each of them wore the same tired expression that I was sure was evident on my own face. For a while, no one spoke and I didn't mind that at all. I knew that when the thin rusted wire finally snapped, the torrent of sordid memories that would pour forth would be tremendous. I could only pray that we would not drown in it.

Chapter 4

"Iris Preston Charged with Murder," Ruth read the headline out loud. "I always thought Bubbie had a crazy streak," Ruth said. "I know I have it."

"I know what you mean," I said, sitting up in the chair. "There's no way we could escape it."

"What are you talking about?" Rand asked, an edge to his voice. "What streak are you talking about?"

"The same one that Mama had," Faye piped up, "And Grandma and all of her family, too. Don't you remember all of those stories about Grandma and how mean she was?"

"Well *I* certainly don't have it," Trevor interjected.

"Oh," I said, "and what makes *you* so damned special? I seem to remember a certain wife left alone in Kentucky, and a certain trashy little girl you drug down here and shacked up with at Christmas, of all times. You took a little vacation from your wife of twenty-three years and spent the whole time boozing and smoking pot, if I remember correctly."

"What has that got to do with anything?" Trevor responded, obviously embarrassed and more than a little pissed off. "That was a long time ago."

"Oh that's right," I said, sarcastically. "I forgot, you suddenly became Billy Graham, *again*, and all was forgotten."

"Sammy, stop it," Rene' said, reaching for her cane, "or I'm leaving."

"Yeah, you're on dangerous ground," Brett said, anger reddening his face. "You weren't exactly an angel before you left for the army."

"I never claimed to be," I said. "At least I had the balls to..."

"Everybody shut up!" Ruth half yelled, startling everyone in the room. "We have shit to take care of here. Serious shit. Shit that we will never handle if we don't get it together."

Silence followed as everyone considered how correct she was. One emotional blow after another was taking its toll on the family and we were all beginning to unravel.

"Have any arrangements been made for Mama's funeral?" Rene' asked.

"Not yet," I answered. "They're going to perform an autopsy tomorrow. As soon as that's done, I'll get in touch with the funeral home. I found her insurance policy. It shouldn't be much trouble."

"Trouble?" Rand asked, with angry perplexity. "It's *trouble* to bury your mother?"

"I'm sorry, Rand," I said, meaning it. "I only meant that everything was under control in that area. Has anyone called Uncle Glenn? He's her only living relative, I think."

"Goodness, Sam, Uncle Glenn died four years ago," Faye said, looking at me as though I was stupid.

"Oh, uh, sorry," I said. "Nobody told me. I guess that's what I get for staying out of touch. So there's nobody else to call. Except maybe the preacher at Harvest Church. There was a message from him on the answering machine asking one of us to call. I don't know how he found out about Mama. I didn't call anybody from the church."

"I called the prayer chain," Faye said. "They needed to know."

"Of course," I mumbled, rolling my eyes at her.

"Don't start, Sam," she warned. "That was her church and they loved her."

"Do we have to have the funeral *there*?" Ruth asked. "Can't we just have it at the funeral home?"

"She would have wanted it at the church, Ruth," Faye answered. "It's just understood."

"Fine," I said, anxious to get passed the gory details. "I'll call Brother What's-His-Name tomorrow. I suppose someone will sing."

"Brother *Duplantis*," Faye said, emphasizing the man's name, "will be glad to take care of all that."

"Good, all that's taken care of," I said, authoritatively. "Now, about Bubbie; I might be able to talk them into letting her post bail. But I'm sure it will be quite a lot and I'll need help." At first no one said anything. Then Brett spoke up.

"I'll help," he said. One by one, everyone pledged that they would help post bail, if it was possible.

"I'm paying for her attorney," I said. "I graduated from high school with Richard Romero. He's already agreed to take her case. He wants to meet with us next week."

"You already took care of that?" Rand asked, astounded. "You were more worried about Bubbie's situation than you were about burying Mama? She *killed* her, Sam!"

Suddenly I leaped up from my chair. "I want you, all of you, to look me in the eye and tell me that you did not feel at least *a little* relief, maybe even *joy* deep down in your heart when you heard that Mama had died," I said, the volume of my voice rising with each word. "Yes, our mother is dead, but Bubbie is still alive. And it's long past time for us to get our heads out of our asses and deal with a few things. And don't pretend that you don't know what I'm talking about." In unison, every head in the room hung miserably. I had touched a nerve that was just as raw for my brothers and sisters as it was for me. "I know you remember. I know you have heard Bubbie's screams replayed in your mind late at night. I have. And I know one thing for sure: Prescilla Preston will never hurt anyone again...with her hands or her words." Everyone looked at me then, understanding written upon every countenance.

"I talked to Richard about it," I said. "And he thinks he can get Bubbie off of this."

"Temporary insanity?" Ruth asked.

"Sort of," I answered. "Post Traumatic Stress Disorder. You know, like with soldiers who return from war and freak out when a gun is fired, or when a car backfires? It's the same thing with Bubbie, hell, with all of us. We had our war. And whether you admit it or not, every last one of us is still dealing with it."

"God, Sammy, you're right," Brett said, his face clouding. "I still wake up at night and hear her footsteps coming down the hall. And on those nights, I have to leave the light on because I just know she's going to come in with the broom and beat me with that plastic hairbrush. To this day I sleep with my hands on top of the covers."

"Why Brett," Rene' asked. I noticed Rand and Trevor shifting uncomfortably in their seats and knew that, like me, they knew exactly what Brett was talking about.

Brett continued, "Because if you had your hands under the covers it meant, well, that you were playing with it. Or with each others'."

"Oh my God," I said, a long suppressed memory suddenly springing up. "The hairbrush. That big ass, black plastic brush. She would take it and..."

"...and pound us on the di--, I mean penis with it," Trevor said, finishing my statement.

"I always wondered," Rene' began, "why the boys would sometimes yell out when she went down the hall in the middle of the night. I always thought you had been caught out of bed playing or something. I think I'm going to be sick."

"Most of the time I would be sleeping," Brett continued, "and would wake up with her beating me with the brush. I peed blood for two days one time."

There was more talk that night of Prescilla's abuse. Once it started there was no stopping it. Each one of us shared stories of days and nights spent in terror, waiting for the dreaded outbursts to take place. Only two seemed to hold back. Trevor and Rand sat there, stone faced, as the rest of us spilled our guts, revisiting our private childhood hells. I'm not sure why they were so afraid. They were even defensive of Prescilla at certain points, making excuses for her. But they would not be able to hold it in forever. Eventually, willingly or unwillingly, they would both have to talk about it. And that time would come sooner than either of them knew.

Everyone stayed at the old house that night and all of us slept well into the following morning. I had just plugged in the old percolator when the shrill ring of the telephone startled me. It was the Martin Parish Coroner's office. The autopsy was complete and the official cause of death, as expected, was respiratory failure brought about by an extreme abundance of diazepam in her bloodstream.

So Bubbie's story was confirmed. She had fed over seventy-five valium to Prescilla, just as she had claimed. I thanked the employee at the coroner's office and hung up the phone, immediately dialing Richard Romero's office. He was out so I left a message for him to call me as soon as possible. Ruth ambled sleepily into the kitchen and I related to her the coroner's findings.

"Well, what do we do now?" Ruth asked, opening the vertical blinds that hung over the patio door. Sunlight streamed into the kitchen, lending a strange cheeriness to the heavy atmosphere, and I actually felt a slight emotional lift.

"I left a message for Richard Romero to call me," I answered. "He'll get the ball rolling. I'm sure jury selection will be shortly forthcoming. Bubbie should go to trial rather quickly. The docket in Martin Parish can't be all that busy. They sent Mama's body to the funeral home in LaSalle. She'll probably be in the same room Rick was in. This all sucks, Ruth. I'm tired and to tell you the truth I wish I had never come back here."

"Well I'm glad you're here," Ruth said. "Believe it or not, your presence here is keeping a semblance of order. Your energy is what we all need. I think it's good that you separated yourself from here. You seem to be more objective than the rest of us."

"I just want to wrap all of this up and get back to my life, Ruth," I said. "I will do anything necessary to keep all this shit from hurting my kids."

"I don't blame you, Sammy," Ruth replied. "They're so carefree. Its obvious they are happy. I envy them. I don't know if I will ever be truly happy."

"Its not too late, Ruth," I said, walking across the kitchen to put my arm around her shoulder. "I just feel that somehow this might help us."

"I hope so, Sam," she answered, "I could sure use some help."

The floor creaked as Faye walked into the room. I relayed the news to her and she immediately telephoned the most Reverend Duplantis to give details about Prescilla's funeral. It would be the following afternoon at the Harvest Church of Bayou Martin. Her body would be displayed at two o'clock in the sanctuary.

One by one, the remainder of the Preston kids came into the kitchen and was informed of all the news and details. We decided to have breakfast at the *Waffles Galore* in LaSalle and were soon dressed. We ate quietly, little conversation passing between us. As everyone left, I remembered that Richard was supposed to call me, and decided to go by his office.

As I walked into the nicely appointed lobby, the receptionist glanced up at me and I recognized her as Chris Chaumont, also a graduate of LaSalle High. After a few brief pleasantries, she showed me in to Richard's office.

"Hello Sam," Richard said, getting up from behind his desk offering a handshake. "Man, it's been a long time."

"Sure has, Richard," I agreed, "But it's good to see you, even under these circumstances."

"I'm so sorry you're going through all of this," Richard said, re-seating himself behind the mahogany desk, opening a humidor and retrieving two cigars. "It must be hard to deal with."

"It's all just fucking crazy, Richard," I said, accepting the cigar and having a seat across the desk from Richard. "I want to get this done as quickly as possible." Reaching across the desk, I handed Richard a check. "This should cover your retainer fee," I said.

"Sam, I wasn't even planning to charge you for this," Richard said, lighting our cigars. "You and I were best friends in high school. I remember your mom very well. Too well."

"Well, I appreciate the gesture, Richard," I said, "but I'm sure the good people of LaSalle don't keep you busy enough to work for free. Keep the check and let me know how much I owe you when all this shit is over with."

"Thanks, Sam," Richard said, folding and pocketing the check. "Times do get lean around here sometimes. If it weren't for our classmates getting divorced or filing for bankruptcy, I'd be broke!"

"So what do we do?" I asked, drawing on the fat cigar.

"First," Richard began, exhaling a pleasantly pungent cloud of blue smoke, "I'm going to schedule an interview for your sister with a friend of mine who is a psychology professor at Louisiana State. He's retired from practice but I know he'll love this. He specialized in post traumatic stress disorder during the late seventies and early eighties, having ample research material available with all the Vietnam vets. I studied under him when I was in college and we became friends. His name is William Parkson and I know he'll be perfect for this. We'll submit his findings as evidence for the defense and have him testify at the trial."

"I trust your judgment, Richard," I said, "anything you say, I'll do."

"Well, now the hard part," Richard said, removing his eyeglasses and wiping them with a handkerchief. "Based on what you have told me about your family life while growing up, as well as what I know about it first hand, I want to do something that you might find a little disagreeable, even upsetting."

"Lord, Richard, what is it?" I asked.

"I want to call on all of you to testify about your mother's abusiveness, Sam," Richard answered.

"Oh, Richard, I just don't know," I said, nervously rubbing the side of my face with my hand. "I could probably get through it but I don't know about my brothers and sisters. We all have our secrets, Richard and we're pretty protective of them."

"I can subpoena them, Sam," Richard said. "They'll have to do it or face contempt charges."

"How in the hell have I ended up in this shit?" I asked, not really directing my question to anyone. "One day I'm walking along the Thames, happily sipping a bloody-mary, throwing bread to the Queen's Geese and the next thing I know I'm in Bayou fucking Martin, Louisiana with a dead brother, a murdered mother, and a sister facing prison. God, Richard, it's just so, I don't know, *white trash*."

"I feel for you, Sam, I really do, but if you want to keep your sister out of prison, then do what I'm suggesting. I wouldn't be proposing any of this unless I thought it would work."

"I'll talk to my brothers and sisters about it. But, you might want to get those subpoenas ready. You'll probably need them. Well, I have to get ready for another funeral, so I need to be going. Thank you for everything Richard. I'll call you in a couple of days."

"Okay, Sam," Richard said. "And tell that hottie wife of yours I said hello!"

"Watch it!" I said, jokingly. "Thanks again."

As I walked out the front door of Richard's office, I glanced across the street at the familiar sights and scenes of LaSalle. The old drugstore was still on the corner of Main and First, elderly patrons hobbling in and out, clutching their small white bags with the big blue Rx symbol on the side. Across from the drugstore was the little patch of grass on which stood an old piece of artillery, boasting a plaque commemorating LaSalle's only World War II hero, old Mr. Geautreaux who had died years earlier. This was Americana at its very best, and I became angry as I took it all in. Angry that I had never been allowed to just be a normal part of this small, uncomplicated life. I had lived in a constant daze as a child and teen, everything plastic and unreal.

And there I stood, years later, my life once again caught up in the whirlwind of shit that had always revolved around my family. And there wasn't a damned thing I could do about it. Not gracefully, anyway. The thought of just quietly driving away to the airport, my wife and children in tow, had entered my mind several times over the course of the previous days, but I couldn't do it. No, whether I liked it or not, and no matter how much distance I put between myself and this place, I was irreversibly involved. And I would remain so to the bitter end.

The next afternoon, Denise and I arrived at the Harvest Church of Bayou Martin at about one forty-five. Josh and Adaire had been through enough trauma, I believed, so we decided to leave them at my father-in-law's house for the next several days. The rest of my family filtered in and by nine all of us were there. As is the usual custom, the casket was opened for the family first and we gathered around it, none of us speaking. Gazing upon Prescilla's lifeless face, I was amazed by its peaceful look. Where deep furrows normally creased her brow there was only smooth skin, and the ghost of a gentle smile seemed to play about her mouth. For the first time, I saw in her dead face the peace that Prescilla had never seemed to obtain in life, and it saddened me.

Most of the denizens of Bayou Martin arrived shortly thereafter, and the sanctuary was soon packed with people, women mainly, who had been Prescilla's lifelong friends. As I sat in the hard pew and listened to the lilting tones of the organ, I recalled the last time I had sat in the Harvest Church of Bayou Martin. It was the year I had left for basic training, and that particular Sunday just happened to be Father's Day. The sermon was from Ephesians -- children obey your parents, the preacher had begun. I remembered bracing myself for the usual lecture of how disrespectful and ungodly children had become since "back in the day when children were seen and not heard", but soon the message transitioned into one of parenting, fatherhood in particular. One verse had caught my attention and remained in my mind for quite some time afterwards.

"Fathers, provoke not thy children to wrath," the preacher had read from the scriptures. I wondered if that verse applied to mothers as well. I had decided that no, it must not.

Several times during my mother's funeral I found myself crying, even sobbing. Despite everything, there remained within me a feeling akin to love for my mother, I realized, even though no such love, however faint, was never reciprocated. As we filed past her casket for a final look, a final goodbye, a mixture of release and pain stabbed my heart. What I had always imagined as an end to my anguish, and that of my brothers and sisters, had not proved to be a conclusion at all. There was only an abysmal void in the space that hurt, confusion, and bitterness had once occupied.

After a short ride to Camp Harvest, we were soon crowded together beneath the meager shade of the dark green funeral home tent, my mother's casket resting on the chrome support frame that held it above her open grave. After a few short words from Brother What's-His-Name, the crowd dispersed and we each went our own way. The acrimonious words that had passed between my siblings and me weighed heavily on my mind as I walked slowly to the van. Never before, even during those several years abroad, had I felt so distant from my family. By her death, albeit an inflicted one, Prescilla had finally realized what she had always seemed to desire. My thoughts were completely taken up by her, her life, and her passing.

Chapter 5

O ver the next couple of weeks, Denise and I visited Bubbie quite often and she seemed to be holding up well. It struck me how serene and even jovial she appeared, sitting there in her cell at the parish jail. Bail had been denied, no surprise. The District Attorney had decided to push for a charge of second degree murder, also no surprise. Bubbie underwent the interview with Dr. Parkson, so all we had to do was wait for arraignment and then trial, and hope that everything would transpire as Richard Romero had said it would.

Denise, the kids, and I returned to mother's house and made it our base of operations. My siblings were in and out on a daily basis, which I found quite pleasant. The more I learned about them and how events in their lives had transpired since I had left home, the more I began to understand just how deeply my mother had affected them. Each of them had battled their demons throughout their lives and they were still battling. I sensed that we were beginning to come together again, our relationships deepening every day.

Richard Romero wanted to meet with all of us, so I invited all of my siblings over to mother's house for dinner. Unsure of how they would react to Richard's plans for Bubbie's defense, I was apprehensive about the evening and found it necessary to insulate myself with that wonderful concoction of tomato juice and vodka that had served me so well over the years. Everyone arrived and after a fantastic dinner prepared by my gastronomically gifted Denise, we all took seats in the den.

As everyone made themselves comfortable, Richard began.

"As you all know by now, I'm Richard Romero. Sam and I were friends during high school and he has asked me to act as defense for your sister Iris. Her trial is scheduled to begin on Wednesday of next week, and I need for all of you to be there. I understand this may be inconvenient and may not be what you had in mind, but to be honest with you, that doesn't matter. I don't know if Sam has discussed anything with you, but I will be calling on each of you to testify at one point or another during the course of the trial."

"Testify?" the voice belonged to Rand. "About what? I wasn't here when...when it happened. What would I have to testify about?"

"Yeah, really," Trevor chimed in. "I don't see why we have to be involved in this."

"She's your *sister*, Trev," Ruth said, disdainfully.

"I think we should all be there," Faye added.

"I realize none of you, except Sam, of course, were there when the incident occurred," Richard continued, "but I need for each of you to testify about what may have led up to what your sister did. I plan to lay out before the jury the real depths of abuse that each of you lived through as children. I can assure you that it will not be easy to endure, but if you want your sister to avoid rotting away in prison for the rest of her life, I suggest that you follow my lead on this and cooperate."

"So you're going to make my mother, my *dead* mother out to be some sort of monster for the whole world to see?" Rand asked, anger reddening his face. "I don't think so!"

"But she *was* a monster sometimes," Renee' said.

"Yeah, but does everyone in the world have to know about it?" asked Faye.

Soon everyone in the room was arguing and bickering, the noise level rising with each angry word uttered. I looked over at Richard and rolled my eyes, motioning toward the kitchen doorway. We slipped quietly into the kitchen and closed the door behind us. Folding my arms and leaning back against the kitchen counter, I sighed deeply and looked helplessly at Richard.

"Well this is what you have to work with, Rich," I said. "I told you it would be a mess."

"Just do what you can, Sam, to make them understand how important they are to your sister's defense," Richard replied, retrieving his car keys from his pocket. "Have fun!"

"Gee, thanks a hell of a lot, Rich," I said, punching him in the arm. "You've got everyone stirred up and now you're going to bail out on me!"

Richard walked toward me and put his arms around my shoulders, embracing me tightly. "Sam, it's going to work out. One way or another, this will *all* work out," he said, pulling away. "I'll need to meet with you again sometime before the trial begins. Give me a call on Monday."

"Will do, Rich," I answered. "Have a good night. And thanks for coming over."

"No problem, Sam," he said, and stepped out the door.

Back in the den, the uproar had died down and as I walked back into the room, everyone turned and stared at me, mixed emotions playing across each face. As I surveyed each of my brothers and sisters, I wondered whether this group of fragile, hurting people would still be intact when all was said and done. It struck me as odd that I, the youngest of the family, was the one standing there, the burden of everyone's expectations weighing so heavily on my already tired shoulders. And then it hit me. They looked to me because I was the one, the only one it seemed, who had escaped.

That realization saddened me and a twinge of guilt tugged at my heart. They had remained, had braved the storm, while I had fled like a scared child. Hell, I had been a scared child when I had left. But I couldn't shake the feeling that I had somehow wronged them, even abandoned them. They were stuck in the web, entwined in the sticky intricacies of their pasts, unable to pull away. But what they didn't know was that I was just as stuck as they were. I had just become extremely adept at pretending that I wasn't.

"Well there it is," I said, stepping down into the den. "Bubbie's trial starts next Wednesday at nine o'clock in the morning. I hope you seriously think about this. Richard meant it when he said he would subpoena all of us. Personally I think it would be a damned shame if he had to do that. I'm going to sit in front of the television now and find something mindless and idiotic to watch. Feel free to stay here if you'd like." With that I plopped down onto the couch, pointed the remote control at the television and surrendered my mind to the shallow, unchallenging world of must-see television. My brain was soon coasting on autopilot and I didn't even notice when one-by-one everyone departed.

Chapter 6

The courthouse in LaSalle, the seat of Martin Parish, was an old building, employing architecture which was supposed to bring to the beholder's mind some Roman construction of old. The inscription above the arched entranceway, "COVRT HOVSE," always provoked a chuckle, at least from me. As Denise and I pushed open the double oak doors and stepped into the lobby, I remembered my last visit there.

It had been the summer of my eighteenth birthday, and my adult life had been about to begin. I had already enlisted in the Army and was spending a lot of time with my friends before I was to leave for basic training. I had developed a certain affinity for marijuana that year and had found myself caught up in a surreal whirlwind of parties and all night binges. Short of cash, a couple of guys and I broke into the LaSalle High School and stole two televisions and three video cassette recorders. After selling the stolen items a few towns away, we bought up enough weed to supply the Democratic National Convention, and stayed stoned for seven days straight.

I left for basic training shortly thereafter and discovered about halfway through the grueling course that without the toxins of alcohol and marijuana, my head had cleared and that I liked it that way. Basic training ended just before Christmas and I was given a two-week leave before beginning the advanced individual training where I would learn my military skill. To be honest, I had completely forgotten about the crime my cohorts and I had committed, convinced that nothing would ever come of it. I was quite shocked when the telephone rang at my mother's house two days after I arrived home for my leave. The Martin Parish Sheriff's Office, having done its job well, had discovered exactly who had broken into the high school, and, being put under a little pressure, the sons of bitches who were supposed to have been my friends had said that the whole thing had been my idea.

The detective on the other end of the line suggested that I just come on down to the Covrt

Hovse and turn myself in -- which I did with little compunction. I was to appear before the judge two days later. Of course my mother was dying from embarrassment and took great pleasure in informing me that she had always known that I was no good, destined for prison or some worse fate.

I wore my army uniform when I appeared before the judge, hoping he would realize that I wasn't the same person who had broken into the school. Audibly, my knees knocked together as I stood there before the foreboding, black-clad man sitting behind the bench.

"Mr. Preston," the judge began, "the crime you committed calls for no less than three years in a correctional facility in the state of Louisiana." Blood drained to my feet and I was afraid for a moment that I was going to fall to the floor. Breaking into a cold sweat, I put my hand on the knob of the railing for support.

"But I don't believe you're a criminal," he continued, a glimmer of hope strengthening my weakened knees. "Son, why you would align yourself with those who were with you in this is beyond me. I'm going to give you the benefit of the doubt here and mitigate this charge to a misdemeanor use of a movable. I further suspend any sentence imposed and since the army will be controlling you better than we can, I'm placing you on two years unsupervised probation. I hope you understand how close you came to prison and further hope that my instincts about you are right." I will never forget the sound of the banging gavel that dismissed us from the court. That had been my one and only brush with the law, and I will be forever grateful to that judge for giving me such a break. Nor will I forget my mother's disappointment at my good fortune.

"Well he sure as hell doesn't know you like I do," had been her only statement as we walked out to the truck. I returned to Fort Jackson early, well before Christmas day. Stealing quietly from the house before daylight one black morning, I had hiked into town to the Continental Trailways bus station, my duffel bag on my back. As I had slumped into the spongy vinyl seat, I stared out of the window as LaSalle slowly disappeared from my view, and at least for a while, from my life.

Denise and I stepped into the small courtroom and walked down the aisle to the row of seats directly behind the table where Bubbie and Richard sat, waiting for the judge to enter. In unison, my brothers and sisters, already seated, turned to look at Denise and me as we squeezed into the narrow seats. Apprehension played across each face, furrowing brows and bringing about much wringing of hands.

Glancing around, I beheld what had to be every member of the Harvest Church of Bayou Martin packed into the small courtroom. The hatred on the faces of those people would have been alarming, had I really cared about them. I had a sneaking suspicion that their collective tune would change when all this was over with, whatever the outcome held for my sister.

Bubbie glanced back at us over her shoulder and I was struck by the serenity that bathed her face. She didn't look at all like a woman who was about to tried for murder. She seemed too calm, too peaceful. Pushing his chair back from the table, Richard Romero got up from his seat and walked back to where I was sitting.

"Well, Sam," Richard began, leaning close to me, "we already have one thing in our favor. The presiding judge is Sandra Holbrook."

"I don't think I've ever met her," I said, not knowing exactly why we were whispering.

"Well number one, she's a woman," he continued. "She also holds a degree in social science. She has won a lot of recognition as an advocate for abused children, Sam. She's just the kind of person we need right now. On the other hand, she's also known for handing down some of the toughest sentences in the state. Let's just hope that your sister's story, as well as those of the rest of you, will strike a sympathetic chord with her."

"That's good to know, Richard," I said, still wondering at my sister's unbefitting degree of composure. "I'll just be glad when this is all over with."

"I know Sam," Richard said knowingly, "but you know the hardest part of this is yet to come. At her arraignment, your sister pled not guilty by reason of temporary insanity stemming from post traumatic stress disorder. Now it's just a matter of making those people sitting in that jurors' box believe that that was exactly the case."

"Well I'm ready," I replied, "and I think everyone else is too."

Richard returned to his seat by Bubbie as the bailiff entered the room and announced that court was in session. As everyone stood, Judge Sandra Holbrook came into the courtroom and took her place behind the bench. She was younger than I had expected, or at least appeared so, and possessed an understated beauty that was disarming and put me somewhat at ease. Probably has a heart of stone, I thought, as I watched her shuffle through the stack of folders on the bench. A feeling of dread coursed through me as the proceedings officially began.

As the prosecution made its opening remarks, I surveyed the jurors, their expressions stony as they listened. I wondered about them, about their lives. What kind of backgrounds did they have? Were they ever abused by a parent, or an uncle, or a teacher? Did they face the demons that Bubbie and the rest of us battled? It seemed unfair, somehow, that my sister's fate rested in the hands of those few, un-remarkable people who by chance happened to be registered voters in Martin Parish. Did they realize the gravity of their task, or did they just want to get it over with and get on with their lives?

Soon the preliminaries were out of the way. The prosecution had stated their charges and the judge had heard the usual first testimonies. The detectives who had investigated the case made their statements as did the coroner who had determined what had ended my mother's life. Bubbie remained calm and attentive throughout the whole day and as quickly as it had begun, court adjourned. All I did was sit there all day yet I still found myself exhausted.

As I watched them lead Bubbie away, I discovered tears welling up in my eyes. She seemed like a child again, being told what to do, and complying with no resistance at all. Maybe she had simply resigned herself to the worst, I didn't know. Whatever the case, I was glad to see her in good spirits. I was learning more each day how truly resilient the soul could be.

The next day, we all gathered once again in the courtroom. Bubbie was just as calm as she had been the day before. Intently reading over some papers, Richard looked back at me and winked. He had retained most of his boyish appearance and I remembered seeing that wink when we were teens. Funny how life can be, I thought. Back when Richard and I were party buds, I never would have imagined that we would be sitting in a courtroom, years later, my sister's fate in his hands.

After the pomp and circumstance and other bullshit was out of the way, Richard called the defense's first witness to the stand. In his dapper suit and round, wire-rimmed spectacles, Dr. Parkson looked quite professional. Placing his hand on the Bible, he took the oath and sat down. Richard sauntered over toward him, smiling briefly at the jury as he went.

"Sir," Richard began, "please tell us your name and your profession."

"My name is Dr. William Parkson. I am a Doctor of Psychology and I teach a graduate psychology class at Louisiana State University."

"Dr. Parkson," Richard continued, "are you familiar with the phenomenon known as post traumatic stress disorder?"

"Yes sir," he replied, "I wrote my thesis on the disorder."

"Can you give us laypeople a brief rundown on exactly what post traumatic stress disorder is?"

Shifting in his chair, Dr. Parkson began, "Well, as the description of the disorder suggests, Post Traumatic Stress Disorder, or PTSD, is a psychological condition experienced by a person who faced a traumatic event, an event outside the range of usual human experience. Events such as war, torture, rape, intense abuse, or natural disaster are all stressors that can lead to PTSD."

"Well Doctor," Richard interrupted, "all of us go through trouble. Divorces, failure at one thing or another, financial trouble; and yet most of us get along just fine."

"You're talking about what psychologists call 'adjustment disorders', which are completely different from the types of stressors that can bring about PTSD," Dr. Parkson explained. "And PTSD has certain indicators that classify it as what it is. A person with PTSD was exposed to a traumatic event that involved threat of death, or some threat to the physical integrity of self. The person responds to the particular event with intense feelings of fear, helplessness or sheer horror. In most cases, the person feels as if the event is happening again. Or some internal cue that represents a certain aspect or symbol of the event can trigger the symptoms of PTSD. Most people try to avoid stimuli associated with the trauma they went through."

"Dr. Parkson, what are some of the symptoms of Post Traumatic Stress Disorder?" Richard asked, pacing back and forth in front of the bench.

"The range of symptoms is quite broad," Dr. Parkson went on. "Withdrawal from society, outlandish behavior, irrational fears, sudden outbursts of anger or violence, these are all symptoms..."

"Wait, go back for a moment, if you would, Doctor, what were those symptoms?" Richard cut in.

"Withdrawal, outlandish behavior, irrational fears, sudden angry or violent outbursts..."

"Stop! Right there," Richard said, curtly. "Violent or angry outbursts. You mean that Post Traumatic Stress Disorder can cause an otherwise reasonable person to lash out in a violent manner, even if they are not predisposed to such actions?"

"Yes, it has been documented in countless cases of persons with PTSD," Dr. Parkson replied.

Richard walked over to the table where Bubbie was sitting and picked up a folder. Leafing through the papers in the folder, Richard walked up to the railing in front of the witness stand. "Doctor, are you familiar with Miss Iris Preston, the woman who is on trial here today?" Richard asked.

"Yes sir, I have met and interviewed Miss Preston," the doctor answered.

"Your Honor, I would like to admit this transcript of Dr. Parkson's interview with my client into evidence for the defense," Richard said, handing the folder he had been holding to the bailiff.

"In your professional opinion, Dr. Parkson, does Miss Preston suffer from this Post Traumatic Stress Disorder?" Richard asked.

"After carefully considering the content of our interview and applying my findings to what I know about PTSD, I would have to say yes, she does indeed manifest the symptoms of the disorder."

"Thank you Dr. Parkson," Richard said, "for your time and your professional help."

Judge Holbrook spoke up. "Would the prosecution like to cross-examine?" she asked.

"Uhm, yes we would Your Honor," Martin Parish District Attorney Dallas Guilbeau stated loudly. The acutely southern, no, *more* than southern, more like *redneck* twang in his voice sounded like something from some low-budget movie about the South. I laughed inwardly as his pot belly pushed against the table as he stood up and waddled to the stand.

Clearing his throat and glancing around the courtroom with a practiced look of smug arrogance on his pudgy face, he turned to Dr. Parkson.

"Doctor," he began, his voice wheezy and squeezed, "I'm sure you have a barrel-load of experience dealing with people whose violence you excuse with this, um, *disorder...*"

"I don't excuse anything," Dr. Parkson interrupted defensively.

"Let me finish my question, please, if you would, Dr. Parkson," the DA cut him off, condescension in his tone. "I'm sure you have worked with people who have been through some pretty terrible events that may or may not have caused them to break the law with some act of violence. I can almost understand that. But this woman, who by her own confession coldly and with malice of forethought killed her mother..."

"Objection, Your Honor," Richard said, standing up. "Unless Mr. Guilbeau has been calling the Psychic Friends Network, I don't think he can establish what was going on in my client's mind. He's not the jury either."

"Sustained," Judge Holbrook answered. "And Mr. Romero, don't be smart-alec in my courtroom."

"Ah, yes ma'am," Richard answered, smiling sweetly at the fat DA.

Mr. Guilbeau continued. "My point is, Doctor that this woman did not fight in Vietnam or any other war. The only reason she has given for her actions is some alleged abuse from her victim that may or may not have taken place over twenty years ago. Do you honestly believe we're supposed to believe that this woman suddenly developed this, uh, disorder after twenty years?" The last word of his question, spelled phonetically would look something like "yee-errs."

"As far as we know, there is no set limit as to the time between the trauma and the symptoms. Especially if the stressors are avoided," Dr. Parkson answered.

"As far as you know?" the DA continued his questioning. "So you're not absolutely sure that reaction to a traumatic event is less likely with the passing of time?"

"Not conclusively sure, but all of our research points to..."

"That's all, Doctor, thank you for you testimony," the DA said, cutting Dr. Parkson off again. "That's all, your honor."

"The witness may step down," Judge Holbrook said, banging her gavel. "Let's have a twenty minute recess."

As people milled about, exiting the courtroom for a cigarette, a coke or some other vice, I scanned the faces of the jurors. They were inscrutable. As impressive as Dr. Parkson's testimony had been, I was afraid that just enough doubt was introduced by the District Attorney to make them dismiss it altogether. Richard walked over and sat down next to me.

"Sam, I'm going to start calling you guys now. Who do you think I should call first?" he asked.

"God, Richard, I don't know," I answered. "I haven't really thought about it. Are you going to call Bubbie?"

"Yes, but not right now," he replied, removing his glasses and cleaning them on his shirt. "I need to save that for later. How about I start with you, Sam? Are you up to it?"

"I'll never be up to it, Richard," I said, "so I guess now is as good a time as any."

"Good then," he said, patting me on the shoulder. "You can do it, Sam, just stay with me and try to stay composed. Although a touch of emotion at the right time will actually help."

"Lord, Richard, it's not an act," I said, a little perturbed.

"I know, I didn't mean to make it sound so cold," he said. "Just go with the flow."

The judge came back into the courtroom and the bailiff called the court back into session. "It's *your* time, Mr. Romero," she said as she adjusted her robe to sit down.

"Yes, thank you Your Honor," Richard said, glancing at me. "I would like to call Miss Preston's brother, Mr. Samuel Preston to the stand." My heart began to pound as I slid out of my seat and walked to the witness stand. As I placed my hand on the bible and repeated the oath, I felt hot drops of perspiration begin to drip from my armpits and slide down my sides. Sitting down, facing the courtroom, I wondered if I would be able to go through with it. Richard approached me and winked, putting me a little at ease. Nervously I sipped on the glass of water so graciously provided.

"Mr. Preston," Richard began, "you grew up in the same house as your sister, didn't you? The same house as all of your siblings?"

"Yes-sir, I did," I replied.

"So you witnessed first-hand some or most of the abuse your mother inflicted upon your sister... and received some abuse yourself..."

"Objection Your Honor!" the fat district attorney exclaimed. "The defendant's mother is not on trial here."

Richard quickly cut in. "I'm simply trying to establish that a pattern of abuse did indeed exist, Your Honor. And I know of no other way than to ask those who experienced it." Judge Holbrook looked pensive as she toyed with a small American flag that sat on a tiny stand on her bench. I had to muffle a giggle as I imagined a small cluster of tiny soldiers in World War II garb clamoring around the tiny staff, hoisting it into the air. I fall prey to such silly fancies when I'm under stress, usually at the most inappropriate moments. Judge Holbrook threw a puzzled glance in my direction before speaking.

"I'm going to allow it," she said, finally. "Overruled. You may answer the question Mr. Preston." The district attorney looked irritated as he plopped his large ass back into his chair.

"Yes, I saw and experienced lots of abuse," I replied, my voice dry and scratchy.

Richard looked at me intently; a look of sympathy in his eyes that only I could see. "Can you give the court some specific incidents that took place? Take your time, Sam, I know it's difficult." He was right. This *was* difficult. Damned fucking difficult. Taking a deep breath, I reached back into my past, allowing my mind to take me there, completely surrendering to the memories that I had avoided for so long.

Chapter 7

S hifting in my seat on the witness stand, I stared past the occupants of the courtroom, fixing my gaze on the Great Seal of Louisiana that hung above the entrance. I suddenly imagined the pelican depicted in the seal regurgitating food into the baby pelicans' mouths and the mental picture turned my stomach. Avoiding looking at any of my family, I began my sordid story.

"My earliest memory of fear involves not a physical assault by my mother, but an emotional one. She would read to us from the bible pretty much every night before we went to sleep. She had chosen Ephesians one particular night, the verse which says that children should obey their parents. The verse reads that there is a promise with that commandment that if you follow it, you will have a long life. As my mother finished reading the verse she put her hand softly on my head, caressing my hair.

'You know what that means?' she had asked, her voice soft and tender. 'If you do anything that makes me angry, God will take you out of this world.'

'Like Elijah on the chariot of fire,' I asked, looking up at her.

'No, son, not like that,' she replied. 'He will take your life because He hates children that make their parents angry.' She leaned forward, kissed me softly on the forehead and got up from where she had been sitting on the side of my bed. 'So just make sure you don't do anything bad that would make Mama mad. I love you. Sleep well.'

"As she turned off the light and left the room I lay there, mortified, begging God not to kill me. I went back over my day, trying to remember whether I had done anything bad, or whether she had become angry with me. I decided that I must have been good because I was still breathing. But just to make sure, I said the words you say when you walk down the aisle at church to Get Saved. I think I was six years old then. Some days later, I'm not sure how many, I dropped a plate in the kitchen and watched in horror as it shattered on the hard tile floor.

"I waited for the inevitable bolt of lightning to strike as my mother yelled, 'Do you have any money? Can you buy another plate, you clumsy turd? Clean it up.' When the lightning didn't come, I realized that maybe death was reserved only for those times when she was really, really mad and not just a little mad like when you broke something, or tracked mud into the house. At any rate, I quietly picked up the broken shards of glass, taking care to not let her see my tears, which might have made her angry enough for God to kill me. I remember praying that night, thanking Him for letting me live.

"There were lots of times like that, when I knew and experienced what I thought the bible meant by the "fear of God." I measured every word and action, hoping that her latest outburst wasn't The One that would do me in. It was only after much thought that I decided to risk my life one sunny afternoon and tell my mother something that had happened at school. I didn't see how it could possibly make her angry. Not at me, anyway.

"It was during recess and our small elementary school would send all the students out onto the playground behind the school at the same time. I think I was in first or second grade when the following happened. I was playing on the monkey bars one afternoon when several of the "big kids" asked me to play a game with them. I hesitated at first. I was usually picked on and called names by my own classmates, even more so by the older kids. But being afraid to say no, I climbed down from the monkey bars and followed them around the side of a small utility shed that stood in one corner of the playground. One of the kids, a fifth-grader named Tommy Malone, scratched a line in the dirt with his shoe and told me to stand on it. He then marked off about ten steps and turned around. The other boys lined up next to him. I was afraid. Afraid to stay there and find out what their game was and afraid to run away.

'Now, fag, open your mouth,' Tommy said. Hesitantly I did as he said. Snorting a glob of snot from his nose into the back of his throat, he hurled the nasty projectile from his mouth. Reflexively, I closed my mouth. The spit-missile hit me on the check, oozing down onto my chin. I remember wanting to vomit. Within seconds he was standing in front of me, raising his fist. He punched me in the face and told me there would be more if I didn't keep my mouth open. Petrified, tears streaming down my face, I stood there, mouth agape as the boys played their sick "game". Each in turn, they spit at me, trying to see who could make it into the goal -- my open mouth. By the time the bell rang, my face was covered with slimy wads of mucus.

'If you tell on us, we'll kick your faggot ass,' Tommy had said as he ran around the corner of the shed. Un-tucking my shirt, I wiped the spittle from my face and went back to class. I endured their "game" during every recess period for four days until I finally got up the courage to tell my mother. When Ronnie Darbonne had been beaten up at school, his mother had come to the principal's office and the kid that did it got expelled from school. I just knew that my mother would do the same and I would be rid of Tommy and his thug friends. God was I ever wrong.

'You *what?*' she said, glaring at me. 'You let them spit in your *mouth?* What in the world is the *matter* with you? Why didn't you stop them?'

'I couldn't, Mama,' I said, sobbing. 'They'll beat me up.'

'Well, what a little sissy you are,' my mother snarled. 'You must *like* it or you'd stop them from doing it.'

'You...could...go to the school and talk to the principal,' I stammered.

'What?' she said, agitation in her voice. 'You think I have time to go up there for every little thing that happens to you? I work like a dog in this house, cooking and cleaning, and what thanks do I get? You can't even stay out of trouble at school.'

"She had confirmed my sneaking suspicion that somehow it really was my fault that the boys at school had done this thing to me. But I wasn't at all ready for what happened next. Squeezing my face roughly between her hands, she positioned her face directly in front of mine, nose to nose, and spit.

'There, you like *that*,' she screamed. 'Maybe you'll get enough and make it stop.' She continued to spit until for the second time that day my face was a wet mess. Afterwards, she sat down at the kitchen table and buried her face in her hands, sobbing wretchedly. 'Go clean yourself up!' she yelled and I ran into the bathroom and washed my face."

The discomfort on the face of every person seated in the courtroom was very evident. I tried to look at my family but just couldn't bring myself to see them. As for myself, I was surprised how detached I felt. It was the same flat sort of feeling that I had experienced a few years earlier while taking one of those new miracle drugs that was supposed to help you quit smoking. I didn't care for the feeling back then. I was willing to put up with the lows in order to feel the highs. And I certainly didn't want to quit smoking.

But sitting there in the Martin Parish Covrt Hovse, the flat line was just fine. Telling the world about my childhood wasn't so bad after all, I thought. Catharsis? Maybe. No, it was more satisfaction than anything else. Satisfaction that everyone in the whole fucking parish would finally know the truth about my mother.

Richard Romero had been standing at the rail while I had been talking, head down, his gaze fixed on the floor. He was expecting the worse, I believe. He looked up at me, directing a welcomed wink my way.

"Sam, I know this is difficult. Hell, it would be difficult for anyone. But I need for you to go on." I took another gulp from the glass of water, cracked my neck (a nervous habit that annoyed Denise to no end) and continued.

"I cannot give a chronological play-by-play of my life, but there are lots of instances similar to what I've already talked about. I'm going to skip most of them. I guess the worst thing that happened was when I..."

I faltered then. The flat line was gone. My stomach was cramping and I feared I was going to shit myself right there in front of God, The Honorable Sandra Holbrook and the rest of the world. Could I actually say it? I didn't think so, but to my disbelief the words were coming out before I could stop them. "...when I was molested by the school bus driver."

Richard jerked his head up sharply, looking at me in astonishment. He immediately realized how he must have looked and regained his composure. "Sam..?" he asked, questioningly. I nodded my head, indicating that yes I could go through with it.

"I don't remember exactly how old I was when it began. But it was after my brothers and sisters left home. I was the last kid to get off the bus and there were several miles between my house and the kid's before mine. We would take turns sitting up on the doghouse, the driver called it, the space to the left of the driver by the window, where the bus controls were located. He would let us pull out the big red button that made the stop signs go out when the bus was stopped to load or unload. We thought it was the greatest thing to sit there and work the buttons.

"One afternoon I was taking my turn sitting on the doghouse and soon I was the only one left on the bus. Before we reached the driveway that led to my house, there was a side road that led through the woods to the river. Without any warning, Mr. Oldeman, the bus driver, turned the bus and headed down the little side road. 'Hey, are we going to the river?' I had asked him. 'Oh, no,' he answered, 'I just need to pee. Won't take but a minute.' He stopped the bus, reached over and pushed the handle to open the doors. 'Don't you need to pee, too?' he asked me. 'No sir,' I answered. 'Aw, come on, it's been a long ride, I bet you need to.' So I climbed down off the doghouse and followed him down the two steep steps and out the door.

"When we were outside the bus, I followed him a short distance to the tree line. I turned away from him and unzipped my pants and tried to pee. He unzipped his pants and began to urinate. I remember looking at him from the corner of my eye. I had never seen a grown man's penis before and I was uncomfortable and disturbed that he was exposing it to me. I was nervous and my heart was beating hard. I didn't need to pee, probably couldn't have even if I had needed to, so I zipped my pants up quickly. He shook his penis a few times and then turned to me, still holding it between his fingers.

'You know, one day you'll have a big one like this.' he said, looking down at it. 'Sometimes there's a little game that only boys play,' he continued stepping closer to me. I remember that it was right in my face by then, so close I could smell the odor of stale urine. 'But nobody can know about it, because it's a secret game. Wanna play it?' he asked. I was very afraid by then, because he was getting erect and I had never seen that before. 'You just have to open your mouth...'

"Your Honor, I'm sorry but, as much as I sympathize with Mr. Preston, I don't see where this has any bearing on this case whatsoever," Mr. Guilbeau interjected, standing up. I was so angered by his interruption that I answered the judge myself.

"Ma'am, it's what happens after all this that's important," I said, throwing a sneer at the DA.

"Mr. Guilbeau," the judge said, "I don't think Mr. Preston would be subjecting himself to all of this if he didn't have a good reason. The witness can proceed, if he feels that he can."

"Well anyone can guess what happened next," I continued. "These little stops for well, oral sex went on for about two weeks. He became increasingly more forceful with his approaches as time went on. He would even reach over and fondle

116

me while I was sitting on the doghouse. Then one afternoon he took my pants completely off. I remember I was wearing some new shorts that my mother had bought for me and they had a button instead of a snap. Anyway, it was after that day that I told my mother what was happening. It was the day that he finally raped me. The day he pushed himself into me and I blacked out from the pain.

"I awoke back on the bus at the end of my driveway. I could feel this disgustingly wet sensation in my pants. I later discovered, while taking a bath that it was blood. His disposition was no longer that of a *buddy old pal* playing a secret game when I got off the bus that day. He was menacing and his face frightening as he told me that if I told anyone what *we did together* he would kill me.

"The blood really scared me and I sat there in the bathtub, crying, debating on whether or not to tell my mother. I finally decided that I had to tell her, because, after all there was blood on me. So after I put on my pajamas, I walked into her bedroom. She was already in bed, reading her bible.

'Mama,' I had said, timidly, walking up next to the bed. She peered at me over the top of her book. 'What?' she answered, flatly. 'Something bad happened on the bus today,' I said, not looking at her.

'Oh Lord, what now?' she asked, sitting upright and swinging her legs over the side of the bed. I almost decided to make up something innocuous, but couldn't think of anything convincing that quickly. 'Mr. Oldeman, he...he did something to my behind...'

'WHAT? What did you do?' she yelled, jumping up out of the bed. 'You didn't *tell* anybody did you?' she screamed. I remember thinking then that Mr. Oldeman had been right. It *was* a secret game that all boys played and that I had violated some sacred vow and that my mother was angry at me, and that this time she was angry enough for God to kill me.

'He put his thing in my behind!' I yelled, through streams of burning tears.

'You let him?' she asked, her face red with rage. 'I just knew it!' she continued, 'you are one of those faggot-boys they talk about in San Francisco. And you're already letting grown men fuck you! Fuck you, fuck you, fuck you...'

"She continued to yell as she picked up the lamp from her bedside table and struck me in the head with it. The shade flew off and the light bulb broke, imbedding tiny slivers of glass in my forehead. She was completely out of control then and she hit me with that lamp until my face and back were both bleeding and I had knots all over my head. She didn't stop until I was almost unconscious. The last thing I remembered was her carrying me to my bedroom and tossing me onto my bed.

"She called the school the following morning and told them I was sick. I stayed out of class for over a week, until she thought the bruises and cuts had healed enough for nobody to notice them. She told me that I could never, ever say anything to anyone about what Mr. Oldeman and I had *done together*, and she had no problem watching me walk up the driveway to get on the bus with him morning after morning. She never said anything to anyone, either.

"The sexual abuse from the old pervert stopped after that. I don't know if he got nervous when I didn't go to school for a week or if it had something to do with a kid named Thad Bertrand moving into a house up the road from us, making him the last to get off the bus. "In either case, I never said a word about it to anyone until today. By the way, Mr. Oldeman still lives in Bayou Martin. And I would be more than happy to see him in prison. I don't care how old he is. I got over the physical abuse soon enough. You know, kids are pretty resilient sometimes. But it took years and years for me to understand that what happened was done *to* me and not *with* me."

The courtroom was quiet and still. Nobody moved. Almost every eye in the room was looking to the floor. Richard Romero broke the silence.

"Sam, thank you for sharing that with us, I know it was difficult. Your Honor, the events in this man's traumatic childhood paint but a small frame in the big picture of abuse that was meted out to this family, including to my client. Over the next few days, if you will bear with me, I would like for that picture to become clearer and more complete with the testimonies of all the Preston children."

Removing her glasses and emitting a tired sigh, The Honorable Sandra Holbrook picked up her gavel. "Unless Mr. Guilbeau would like to cross-examine, court is adjourned until next Wednesday at 9:00."

"The prosecution would not prefer to do so at this time, Your Honor," the fat DA said, averting his eyes from mine.

"Very well," the judge said and landed the gavel with one sharp knock.

Chapter 8

It had been a very long time since I had thought about Mr. Oldman and his secret game. I was exhausted from thinking and talking about it and all I wanted to do was go home, take a long shower, drink a beer and go to bed. Well that didn't happen. As we drove up the driveway to the old house, I noticed an unfamiliar car parked just outside the fence. Sitting in the front porch swing, a very small, very gray woman was watching us as we walked up the sidewalk. As we neared her, I recognized her as Miss Kat Thompson, a woman from Bayou Martin who had been one of my mother's closest friends.I had no idea what she wanted and to be honest didn't care to see her or anyone else for that matter. As we walked up the steps onto the porch, she got up from the swing.

"I'm sorry I didn't get to speak to you at your mother's funeral, Sammy," she said, feebly. "But I have some things I need to say to you."

"Miss Kat, I appreciate your coming all the way out here, but honestly, I'm very tired and not up to a visit," I told her, trying not to sound terse. The old woman then began to cry softly as she sat back down on the swing.

"Oh, I knew it was a mistake coming out here," she said. "But I just have to tell you some things about your mother. Some things that might help you to understand, maybe just a little, why she was the way she was." Denise was the next to speak.

"Look, Sam, I was planning to go to Mom's to get Josh and Adaire anyway. Why don't you go ahead and visit for a while." The look she gave me indicated that I would indeed visit with Miss Kat and in no way further upset the poor woman.

"Miss Kat, would you like some coffee?" I asked, offering my hand to help her up from the swing. Her face brightened a little as she nodded her head. Denise went back to the van and I walked my unexpected (and still a little unwanted) visitor into the house. I pulled a chair out from the kitchen table and sat her down, then proceeded to make a pot of coffee.

"I'm sure you're wondering what brought this visit about, Sammy," she said, staring down at her twiddling thumbs. Without looking back at her, I answered.

"To tell you the truth, at this point, I don't wonder much anymore about anything. So just spit it out." I was surprised at the ugly tone of my voice. But this woman was one of them. She was a permanent fixture at the Harvest Church of Bayou Martin and just for that I hated her. And I hated myself for feeling that way. Handing her a cup of coffee, I tried very hard to smile as I took a seat across the table from her. She accepted the cup with an ancient shaking hand and set it on the table. Gazing wistfully into her cup of coffee, she began to speak.

"I grew up with your mother. She was sixteen years old when her family moved out here to Bayou Martin. Her father, your grandfather, had been a big wheel at a steel company in Mississippi." She paused a moment to take a sip of coffee and dab a napkin daintily at the corner of her mouth. All that done, she continued.

"I can still remember the first day Prescilla walked into our classroom. She looked as though she had just stepped out of a band box. Beautiful and sophisticated, she was. And we were all taken by her right away. She had an air about her that was just lovely. Her dresses were obviously new. Most of us from Bayou Martin were poor and we were just in awe of this new girl.

"Within a few days, Prescilla and I had become friends. I can still remember the first day I visited her out at her house. It was a lovely home, filled with all kinds of nice things. They even had one of those new kerosene stoves I had seen in the Sears and Roebuck. But the neatest thing was the piano. It was the first time I had ever seen a grand piano up close like that. We sat together many evenings in front of that piano playing little duets that we made up as we went. Your grandmother, a beautiful woman herself, would serve us little cookies and cups of tea on a tray.

"I spent many wonderful times out there at the house. I was just as upset as Prescilla was when it burned to the ground one winter's night. It was the kerosene stove. Something had gone wrong with the workings of the thing and it blew up. They lost everything, they did. Their clothes, their furniture, even that wonderful piano. Of course Prissy, that's what we called Prescilla back then, was devastated. And so was her mother. With no belongings and nowhere to live, Prissy, her parents and her brothers and sisters moved in with Prissy's grandparents, her mother's folks. I believe that was the beginning of the end for Prissy's parents. Your grandmother took to drinking and staying out late. She had never really wanted to move here from Mississippi anyway and what with the house burned and all of her fine things gone, she sank deeper and deeper into despair.

"Your grandfather promised to build a new house, and even laid the foundation for it, but that didn't help matters. Within the year, they were divorced. Your grandfather never quite got over it and when he died of a heart attack two years later, everyone believed it was indeed a broken heart that had killed him. The winter the house burned down was the year of my seventeenth birthday, and your mother's as well. Your grandmother left town and didn't return for several years. Prissy stayed here in Bayou Martin with her father and helped care for her brothers and sisters until one day at the post office she met a dashing young man -- Mr. Winston Preston -- your father."

I got up and grabbed the coffee pot, topped off both our cups and sat back down with Ms. Kat, completely entrenched in the story by then.

"Please go on, Ms. Kat," I said, anxiously awaiting more. My mother had never talked much about her past and, to my surprise, this unexpected foray into her life had me completely transfixed.

"Your father had just returned from The War and Prissy fell for him head over heels. They courted a few months and before Prissy turned eighteen, they were married. Winston built the cutest little house for them in Bayou Martin proper with wood he milled himself. Within the year your eldest brother was born and shortly after, another child, your sister Ruth came along. Not even a year later, Rick and Rand were born -- twins run in your family, you know. It was at about that time that Winston took a job working with the Missouri Pacific Railroad..."

Ms. Kat stopped for a moment to take a sip of coffee. She seemed hesitant to continue, a sad look clouding her face. "That was when all the trouble started."

"What kind of trouble?" I asked, wondering what this was leading up to.

"Well," she continued, "when a man worked on the railroad back then, he would be gone for days, sometimes weeks at a time. A young mother, a young woman in her prime, could get lonely, Sammy. Really lonely..."

126

"Oh crap," I said, sitting up. "My mother had an affair?"

"Not just an affair," the old woman continued. She was leaning forward a little, her tone low and her expression that of a woman sharing a really juicy tidbit of gossip for the first time. "There was a family named Thibodeaux. They were, well what we always referred to as 'white trash', if you'll pardon the epithet. They lived in an old farm house out by the river. They were definitely from the wrong side of the tracks and not the sort of people Prissy would have ever been seen with. But one of the boys, Randall, was strikingly handsome and Prissy found herself smitten with him. She had taken the kids for a swim at the river, which was common on a hot day back then, and that's where she met him.

"Well one thing led to another and one day Prissy came to me, so distraught she could hardly walk. She told me that she was pregnant. And that it was Randall's. I did the worst thing I've ever done in my life then, Sammy. I told her to just shut up and not tell anyone. I told her to make sure she was with your father when he came home, let him leave for work, and then tell him about the baby when he again came home. That way he would never know. We were still just kids, Sammy, barely into our twenties. I know it was wrong to tell her to lie, but back then, women just didn't get pregnant for men who weren't their husbands.

"Prissy took my advice and when Renee' was born, it never entered your father's mind that the child was anyone's but his own. Prissy had gotten off Scot free as far as Winston was concerned. But Randall was another story. He knew the child was his, but Prissy begged and pleaded with him to keep quiet about it. He would, he said, but only if Prissy continued to see him when Winston was away with the railroad. Prissy didn't have a problem with that. She was in love with Randall, but didn't want to be a disgrace and didn't want to hurt Winston either. She cared for Winston, but Randall...Randall was the love of her life. And when she found herself once again pregnant with Randall's child, she continued the same charade as before. Your father was none the wiser when the second set of twins were born."

"Oh, God, wait a minute," I said in disbelief. "Are you telling me that Renee, Brett and Bubbie don't belong to my father? Are you sure? How did a whole community keep it a secret?"

Ms. Kat averted her eyes and continued, ignoring or not even hearing my questions. "And then Faye came along..."

"Holy shit, Ms. Kit, uhm, excuse my language, but Faye, too?" I asked, incredulous.

"It was after Faye was born that something happened to change everything. Prissy couldn't take it anymore. She had attended a revival service at the Harvest Church one Wednesday night and well, saw the error of her ways. She broke off the love affair with Randall. She told him she never wanted to see him again, that God himself had told her she was wrong. I think at that time she was even considering coming clean with your father. Well Randall was heartbroken, to say the least. He drove off in his old jalopy truck to the river, first stopping to buy a package of beer, and in a drunken stupor, drove the truck head-on into an oak tree out by the river. He died instantly.

"When Prissy heard that Randall was dead, she went to pieces. Winston was home at the time and couldn't imagine what was wrong. Overcome by emotion and grief, Prissy took to the bed and wouldn't get up. She just lay there sobbing and crying for days until finally Winston put her in the car and drove her to the clinic in LaSalle. It was in the clinic, in the midst of a nervous breakdown that she finally confessed everything."

"What in the hell did he do?" I asked. The whole story seemed unreal, as though it were a plot in an old movie.

"When Prissy came home from the clinic two days later, Winston told her that he wished he would have 'pinched the little bastards' heads off' when they were born. I know he didn't really mean it. Your father was the kindest man I'd ever known. An argument ensued and Prissy gathered up hers and Randall's children and left. She told Winston he could keep his kids and she would take hers. Nobody knows for sure where she went, but a month later, destitute, she came back to Bayou Martin and knocked on the door of the house your father had built for them. She wanted to come home and Winston, being the sort of man he was, sought counsel from his parents. His mother told them that if he really loved her, and he did, that he should take her back and raise the kids as his own. Well, you're here, Sammy, so you can figure out that he did indeed take her back. They had the house, this house we're sitting in now, moved out here to the country. I think you father wanted to get away from all the talk in Bayou Martin.

"As time went by, things settled down. You came along and like the last redeeming chapter of a sad story, put an air of finality on the whole thing. Things went well for a long time until another blow struck Prissy. A group of men from the steel plant where your father worked drove up to the house one afternoon to tell her that your father had been killed when a cable snapped off a crane and struck him in the head. It was then that your mother began to change, Sammy. She began to obsess with the church. And the stronger her obsession became the angrier and meaner she seemed to grow. I don't know, Sammy, if this makes you feel any differently about your mother. All of us kind of knew that she was mistreating you kids, and if you could ever find it in your heart to forgive me, please try. I know what I've shared with you doesn't excuse your mother's actions, but maybe it can explain them some."

I was exhausted and my mind was reeling from the sudden deluge of information that Ms. Kat had found it so necessary to relate. I didn't know whether to thank her or choke the life from her old withered body.

"Have you told anyone else in my family about this, Ms. Kat?" I asked.

"Oh no," she said, feebly shaking her head. "And I won't. You know now and you can do with it what you want."

The old woman seemed relieved, as if a great weight had been lifted from her hunched shoulders and she got up from the table. "I won't keep you any longer."

I let her leave without saying goodbye or even getting up from the table. All I could do was sit and stare through the window at her as she hobbled to her car and pulled off down the driveway. Lost in thought, I got up, went into the den and plopped down on the couch, absent-mindedly reaching for the television remote control. What the hell was I going to do with this, I thought.

Chapter 9

I wasn't sure whom Richard had decided to call next, which was probably a good thing. When he called Ruth to the stand, I was nervous for her, knowing how I had felt a few days earlier. After the usual "state your name for the record" business, Ruth began her recounting of what her childhood had been.

"It's been many years since I was a child," she began, "so I can't really recall everything that took place. I've spent most of my life trying to forget. But there are a couple of incidents that I will never be able to forget.

"When I was in high school, my best friend was a Catholic girl named Rhonda. Well, we weren't allowed to mix with pagan Catholics, as my mother would call them, and even the principal, a member of Harvest Church, kept a close watch. One day

Rhonda and I put on makeup after gym class. I wasn't allowed to wear it, even as a teen, so it was a neat experience. Well, throughout the day, I forgot about it and still had the makeup on my face when I got home. Mama noticed it right away. She had already received a telephone call from the school principal (he had called to tell her that I was hanging around a pagan Catholic), so she was already fuming. She called me a 'painted up whore' and dragged me into the bathroom by my hair. She had grabbed a steel wool pad from the kitchen...and she scrubbed the makeup from my face with it.

"Needless to say, my face was raw and bleeding," Ruth said, crying by then. "There were several patches of raw skin and of course I had to clean up and dress the wounds by myself. I still have tiny scars on my face from that evening. Rhonda cried when she saw me the next day. She thought it was her fault that Mama had done that to me. I made her promise not to tell anyone." Ruth had a distant look about her as she shifted in her seat and took a sip of water. Clearing her throat she began to speak again.

"One afternoon, my brothers Rick and Rand and I were playing near the bayou that ran behind our house. I was about ten years old then.

It was hot that day and before we knew it we had stripped down to our underwear and jumped in. We swam for a little while and then got out and put our clothes back on. When we went back up to the house, Mama noticed right away that our hair was wet but our clothes weren't. She immediately began to rant at me, asking me what I had done as she drug me into the house and then into the bathroom. She made me strip off my clothes and get into the bathtub. She then began to switch me on my back and face with an old plastic flyswatter, telling me that I was going to hell for having sex with my own brothers...and then said...for sucking their cocks. I didn't even know what 'cock' meant when I was that age. I went to bed completely confused that night, feeling ashamed of myself and not really knowing why. It wasn't until years later that I understood what she meant. I hated her. And I'm glad the bitch is dead."

Ruth's last statement took me and every else in the courtroom by complete surprise. A low mumbling resounded throughout the chamber as people reacted to Ruth's impassioned statement. Judge Holbrook had to bang her gavel a couple of times to restore order as she instructed Ruth to please refrain from using profanity in her courtroom. Richard quickly approached the stand.

"That'll be all, ma'am," he said, a little shocked himself at her words. "Thank you for your testimony." Ruth stepped down and returned to her seat.

Chapter 10

My siblings and I were sitting around the kitchen table in the old house, a fug of cigarette smoke hanging in the air. Secretly, I took pleasure in seeing the blue billows wafting through the air, because my mother had always opposed smoking, especially in the house. I toyed with the cup of coffee sitting in front of me, debating about whether or not I would completely change four of my siblings' lives forever or keep my mouth shut and not let them know that our mother had been a .....

"Mama was a whore," I said, the words escaping my lips before I could stop them. Everyone in the room stared at me, a mix of amusement and shock evident on each face. "I mean, well, err, she used to be," I stammered. "Oh crap, never mind," I said getting up from the table and walking toward the den.

"Hey, wait a minute. Come back here!" It was Ruth's voice. "What in the world is the matter with you?"

I turned around and looked around the room, my gaze lingering a little longer on Rene', Faye, and Brett. Everyone eyed me, waiting for me to say something.

"There's something I need to tell you," I said. "Something I found out today. I don't want to, but you need to know. Crap. Crap. How do I say this?" I said, my stomach churning.

"Does it have anything to do with Mama being a whore?" Faye asked innocently. This struck me as extremely funny and I burst into maniacal laughter. Everyone else thought it hilarious as well, except for Faye, that is. I had to sit down and compose myself before I could continue.

"I received a visit today from Ms. Kat Thompson," I began. "She told me that our mother had an affair when she and Daddy were very young. She also told me that Rene', Brett, Bubbie and Faye don't belong daddy, that they belong to some old white trash from up the road who was killed in a car accident."

Well, it was out. I had said it. I looked around the room at the looks of disbelief and anger.

Taking a deep breath, I recounted the entire story the old woman had shared with me.

"Well, I certainly don't believe it!" The voice was Faye's. That's the stupidest thing I've every heard."

"Well if it's true, it certainly would explain some things," Ruth said. "Like why Mama always referred to Renee' as her punishment from God. I always wondered what she thought she was being punished for."

"What do you mean, punishment from God," I asked.

"Well," Ruth continued, "There were lots of times, when Renee' was a child, that Mama would get this really strange look on her face when she would look at Renee'. I remember Mama saying things like, 'I deserve it, Lord, I deserve it. I sinned, I sinned.' I never really thought much of it, because Mama was always saying crazy things. But now I understand."

"Mama considered me to be a punishment from God for her having an affair?" Renee' asked, a look of amused incredulity on her face. "Well that makes me feel great."

"Renee', you know it's not true," Faye said, caressing Renee's arm. "You were a blessing, not a punishment."

"So all those years, she kept this affair hidden," Trevor said. "But what about the rest of the town? They had to have known. How could she have hidden it from the whole town?"

"The whole town did know," Rand answered. "Mrs. Whaler, the Sunday school teachers, and our teachers at school…they all knew. And they knew everything else as well. Don't you remember how everyone always seemed to look at us with some unexplained pity in their faces? I used to think it was because Daddy was killed. But no, it was because they knew what was going on in the Preston house. And they didn't do shit about it, did they?"

This small outburst from Rand was the most he had said at one time since I had arrived in Louisiana. I was glad to hear him talking. Rand was a mystery to me and always had been. He and Rick had always been somewhat exclusive in their relationship, always seeming a bit conspiratorial when they were together. I guess it came from being twins, but I was always envious of their bond. These mysterious men were more like uncles to me, really, than brothers. By the time I had turned ten years of age, they had already left home. Rand eventually married, but Rick never found himself able to commit. Because he was so tight-lipped, I really had no idea what Rand had gone through as a child.

"I've been trying to think about what I will say when the lawyer calls me to the stand," Rand said, absentmindedly doodling on a napkin. "I mean, I wanted to die when I was listening to you, Sammy. I was angry, not only at Mr. Oldeman and Mama, but at myself."

"There's no need..." I began, but was cut off by Rand.

"No, Sammy, let me finish," Rand continued. "I knew what you were going through at home, but I guess I just wanted so badly for it *not* to be true, I convinced myself that Mama had somehow changed over the years, that maybe she was too old to do the same things to you that she had done to us. And of course I had my own children to worry about."

"Rand, really, there's no need to feel guilty," I said, meaning every word. "Even after you left home, you were still her victim. All of us were."

"Well, I hope you forgive me, anyway," Rand continued.

"Of course, Rand," I said, "but only if you can forgive me for staying out of touch for so long."

"I'll have to think about it," Rand said, a scowl darkening his face. I was about to believe he was serious when he broke into a grin. Everyone around the table began to chuckle and for the first time that evening, the oppressive atmosphere lightened, if ever so slightly.

Chapter 11

The following week, Bubbie's trial continued. I had no idea who Richard planned to call to the stand, and I was nervous as I sat once again in the Martin Parish Covrt Hovse. Everyone involved in the proceedings was pretty much seated where they had been during previous days, but I noticed that there were empty seats this time. How typical of these people, I thought. How easily people lose interest when news becomes old news. The extremely short attention span of modern Americans, even those living in rural Louisiana astounded me. The good people of Bayou Martin were probably sitting in their living rooms on their fat redneck asses entertaining themselves with some inane drama about sisters fucking each other's husbands or some equally disgusting talk show fodder. Good for them, I thought, let them forget about the Preston family.

I wanted to think that they were staying away because of their own shame at having abandoned us, passively assisting Prescilla in the abuse she inflicted upon us by failing to intervene all those years ago. But I knew better. They had simply moved on to something newer, more deliciously controversial and trashy. Fuck them.

"Your Honor," Richard spoke to the judge, "I would like to call to the stand…" My heart raced with anticipation. "…Miss Iris Preston." The few non-family members who were attending the trial mumbled in surprise, and I must admit, I was taken aback myself. I had expected Rand or Brett to be called. Maybe Richard had changed his mind. I watched with utter sadness as Bubbie rose from her seat and walked to the witness chair. She didn't seem nervous at all. Hell she almost seemed to skip to the stand. For some reason, her lightness bolstered my paltry feelings even more.

After taking her oath, Bubbie sat down in the chair. Richard took his place in front of her. "Miss Preston," Richard began, "I am going to ask you to talk about some things that you are going to find difficult to share. Do you understand?"

"Yes sir," Bubbie answered, seeming more childlike than ever before.

"I just want you share with us, Miss Preston, what it was like for you when you were a child living with your mother and your brothers and sisters, specifically, your relationship with your mother."

For a moment, Bubbie's face clouded, and I was afraid she would not be able to go through with it, but then she looked out upon the courtroom, a look of resolve on her face.

"Well," she began, clearing her throat, "my childhood was not easy. I was a shy child, and did not really make friends that easily. I had my brothers and sisters at home, and they were the only friends I really had. That's why it's difficult for me to talk about my childhood, because I kept so many things from them. I just didn't want them to know, because their own lives were so difficult back then."

"What things did you keep from them," Richard asked, stepping closer to the rail that surrounded the witness stand.

"Well they all know about most of the things our mother did to me," Bubbie continued, "but there are some things that are just so horrible that people just keep them locked away. One thing that I have never shared with anyone," Bubbie stopped for a moment, visibly shaking," is what happened the week I first started having a period."

An acute wave of nausea washed over me. I did not want to hear what Bubbie had to say about that event in a girl's life that, in a functional family, would usher in a natural transition to womanhood. In the Preston family, there had been nothing functional or natural. Bubbie's story would only add more horror to an already horrible situation. But I knew that I needed to hear it. We all needed to hear it.

"I thought I was dying. I was eleven years old and I had just come home from school. My stomach had been cramping for several days, but I just thought it was a stomach ache, so I just took Pepto Bismol and kept it to myself. Anyway, I had just come home from school and I went to use the bathroom immediately upon arriving at home. It was then that I saw the blood in the toilet and on my underwear. I was so scared that day. I just knew that I had contracted some terrible disease and was dying from the inside out. Mama was outside that afternoon, hanging up sheets to dry on the clothesline in the back yard. I had wadded up some toilet paper and put it in my underwear to keep the blood from staining my clothes even more. I went outside to meet Mama, to tell her what was happening.

"When I approached her, she looked down at me and said 'what do you want.' I almost ran back into the house without telling her about the bleeding, but my fear compelled me to tell her. 'I, I think there's something wrong me,' I told her. I have blood coming from my bottom.'"

When I heard Bubbie say those words, I remembered my own horrible experiences with Mr. Oldeman, and with our mother, on that day that I, too had come home bloody and afraid. At least, I thought, trying to lend some rationality to the whole sad spectacle, Bubbie's condition had been a normal part of life. Yet I could still empathize completely with the fear that she had felt that day at the clothesline with Mama.

"As soon as the words had left my mouth," Bubbie continued, "she clamped her hand over my mouth, glancing nervously around, apparently afraid that someone had heard. She then told me to go into her bedroom and wait. And she warned me to keep my mouth shut and not tell anyone else about it. I couldn't imagine what in the world was going on and why she seemed to be so mad at me. But she was just confirming what I had known all along: that I had done something wrong to make myself bleed from my bottom.

"Well, I went into her bedroom and waited. After about fifteen minutes, she came into the room and closed the door behind her. I guess the other children were outside, because I don't remember hearing anyone in the kitchen. She told me to take off my pants."

An air of abject unease permeated the courtroom. I was becoming progressively sick to my stomach, and I couldn't even think of looking at my brothers or sisters. I couldn't look at Bubbie either. I just sat there with my head in my hands, waiting to hear about what that evil woman had done to Bubbie that day.

"Well, I didn't want to take off my pants," Bubbie said, "but I knew that it would only evoke anger from her, so I did as she said. So there I stood in her bedroom, naked from the waist down, I was holding the crumpled wad of blood-soaked toilet paper against myself, my blood and my shame exposed. 'Yeah I see it,' my mother had said as I stood there in the warm bands of sunlight that striped my body as it streamed in through the thin slits of the window blinds, 'you got your period…your curse. Now boys are gonna want to put their things in you and make you pregnant.' Well I had read a couple of pages about reproduction in a medical book into which I had snuck a peek at the doctor's office one day, so I wasn't really surprised at the act, but it was the way she made it sound so horrible that confused me.

"Then Mama got this sort of pensive look on her face and I could tell that some idea had begun to form in her mind. I remember being utterly afraid at that moment, because I had seen that look on Mama's face before, and it usually heralded some sort of craziness on her part.

"She began to smile as she looked first at my bloodied bottom and then at my face. 'Well we don't have to worry about boys putting their things in you, do we,' Mama had said. 'Yes, yes, we'll make sure they can never do it. Now get on the bed for Mama - '

Bubbie abruptly stopped speaking. She was staring absently at the glass of water sitting on the little table in front of her chair. She was slowly wrapping and unwrapping one lock of her hair around her finger, and her face showed the strain that the relation of these events was placing on her already fragile mind.

"Miss Preston, are you okay?" Richard asked, sincerely concerned for the struggling woman.

Apparently oblivious to Richard's question, Bubbie began to speak again, as abruptly as she had stopped.

"So I got on the bed, and Mama walked over to her chest of drawers. From the top of the chest of drawers, she picked up a washrag. She laid out the washrag on the bed and rolled it into a tube shape, making a crude tampon. She told me to spread my legs and to move the toilet paper out of the way. Well, she tried to push the rag into my vagina. Of course, I had never had anything inside of it before, so the bulk of the rag just wouldn't go in. 'Well that won't do, will it,' Mama had said, and she went again to the chest of drawers and retrieved her hairbrush. She held the bristles in her hand so that the handle was facing out and well, she used the handle to force the rag into my vagina. When I began to scream, she put one hand firmly over my mouth while she continued to force the rag into me using the brush handle. 'Shut up,' Mama said, through angry clenched teeth, 'do you want your brothers and sisters to know that you have a curse on you? Do you want them to know that boys can put their COCKS in your hole now? Maybe you want to, don't you, maybe you want your brothers' cocks in your hole, I know you're thinking it.'

"I remember trying to say no, but couldn't because her hand was still smashing my mouth closed. I could taste blood from the ruptures she caused on my lips. All I could do was to try not to writhe about, as moving around made the already unbearable pain in my crotch even worse. To my horror, Mama wasn't finished. 'Well we will just make double-sure that you can't let a boy put his cock in you, won't we. Oh no, we can't have you going around FUCKING every boy you see, can we you little whore.' The washrag was completely inside me at that point and I was relieved when she moved her hand from my mouth and pulled the brush handle out. I can still remember the pain vividly. But my relief was short lived when she once again returned to the chest of drawers. This time she came back with a wide roll of gray duct tape, the heavy kind. She tore off one long strip, and starting at my navel, covered my vagina with a strip of tape, the way someone might repair a torn piece of vinyl on an old sofa. She continued until she had completely sealed my genitals with tape. And then she abruptly stopped. She had a look on her face as though she had just heard someone calling her name, and she casually left the room without saying a word to me. I waited a few minutes to see if she was going to return, and when she did not, I put my clothes back on and cleaned off the bed. I returned the roll of duct tape to the top of the chest of drawers, and stole quietly down the hallway to the bathroom. I knew that what Mama had done was wrong, I mean, nobody can live with themselves taped up like that, so I removed the tape. I can still remember the pain as the tape pulled out my newly sprouting pubic hair. But the most painful part of the whole thing was when I pulled the rag out of myself. I knew that I was risking further anger from my mother by undoing what she had done, but I didn't care at that point.

"I had already decided that I would not tell anyone about the incident, but there remained the problem of the period itself. Somehow, through Mama's twisted explanation of things, I had realized that the bleeding meant that I could have children, and in spite of everything that had happened that day a wave of excitement coursed through me when I realized that I could become a mother.

"That night I told Ruth about my period and the first thing she asked was whether or not I had told Mama about it. I lied and told her that no, I had not. Ruth advised that I just keep it to myself. She retrieved some sanitary napkins from her dresser drawer and explained to me how to use them. She told me that she got them from her friend's mom every month, and that she would get enough for me too. I was grateful for my sister that night in a way that I had never been before. Mother never again mentioned my period or the incident that had taken place in her bedroom. I promised myself that year that I would explain everything about menstruation to Faye and Renee, and for them to tell me or Ruth about it when it happened.

"I can't really remember anything else about that particular incident," Bubbie said, indicating that she was ready to stop talking about it.

"That's fine, Miss Preston," Richard said. "Your Honor, I have no more questions for Miss Preston at this time."

"Would the people like to cross-examine at this time?" Judge Holbrook asked, looking at the rotund District Attorney.

"Yes we would, Your Honor," the DA replied as he rose from his chair and approached the witness stand.

"Miss Preston," he began, his southern hick drawl seemingly more pronounced than ever. "Did you ever tell anyone about this assault that you allege your mother committed against you?"

"No, I was too embarrassed to tell anyone," Bubbie replied.

"So aside from your account of this incident, there's no proof, no kind of evidence you have to offer that would support this far-fetched story?"

"No sir, I don't have any direct proof that she did it to me. But why on God's green earth would I make up something like this? Do you think I would put myself through this hell if I didn't have too?"

"Please, Miss Preston, it was a just a yes or no question," the DA said. "And yes, honestly, I believe that you are indeed capable of creating a story like this in order to save yourself from going to prison. Tell me, Miss Preston, about the things that you wrote in your personal diary about your mother."

"I wrote lots of things about her in my diary. Which particular passage are you talking about?" Bubbie asked

"This one," the DA said, dramatically pulling a stack of papers from a folder and handing it to Judge Holbrook. "Your Honor, the people would like to introduce this evidence that shows that Miss Preston, with great presence of mind, intended and planned to murder her mother.

"Miss Preston," the DA continued as he handed one of the papers to Bubbie, "is this an entry from your diary, made in your own handwriting?"

"Yes it is," Bubbie replied, perusing the paper.

"Please read for us the entry into your diary, admittedly made in your own handwriting that is dated July 21, 1979."

Bubbie cleared her throat and began to read.

"I have decided that one day I will kill her. It will happen when nobody expects it. I'm not sure when, or how I will do it. I only know that I will do it one day. God forgive me for this, but I will never truly feel alive until she is no longer drawing breath, and is rotting in the ground."

"Miss Preston," the DA said, "how alive do feel now?"

Bubbie started to say something, but the DA stopped her. "You don't have to answer that. We can all see that unlike your mother, you are alive."

Richard threw a glance at me, and I understood from the oh-shit look on his face that he had not seen the diary. I didn't know how the DA had gotten hold of it either. Richard rose from his chair and addressed the judge.

"Your honor, may the defense see this so-called evidence?"

"Make it quick Mr. Romero."

"Your Honor, I don't see anything in this diary entry that says that Miss Preston intended to murder her mother. I don't see the name Prescilla on this paper anywhere. In fact, I don't even see the words mother or mama. This is by no means proof that Miss Preston was writing about her mother."

"Mr. Romero, please," the fat DA retorted, "who else would she be writing about? It is very obvious that she, as well as her siblings hated their mother and wanted to see her dead."

"Objection, Your Honor," Richard quickly interjected. "The prosecution is putting words in my client's mouth, as well as in the mouths of her siblings, who may I remind you, are not on trial here."

"Sustained," the judge said. "The jury will disregard the prosecution's last statement."

"Okay then," the DA said, obviously perturbed. "Just who were you writing about in that diary entry, Miss Preston. And may I remind you that you are under oath."

Without the slightest hesitation, Bubbie looked directly into the prosecutor's eyes, and with the same emotional flatness I had seen in her the day Prescilla died, she replied, "I was writing about my mother."

Exasperated, Richard sat down and put his head in his hands. I wasn't sure what all this was going to mean to the jury, but I was sure it couldn't help matters.

"Nothing further, Your Honor," the DA said.

"Mr. Romero?" the judge said.

"I would just like to ask Miss Preston one more question," Richard answered.

"Miss Preston, try to think back to the day you wrote that entry into your diary. What was it that made you feel the way you did that day?"

"It was the day I lost my baby," Bubbie replied.

Baby? I thought? What baby? I didn't know Bubbie had ever been pregnant. And judging by the faces of my siblings, they hadn't known either.

"I had a miscarriage that morning," Bubbie continued. "I had become pregnant for a married man with whom I worked at the grocery store in LaSalle, after I had moved out of mother's house to live with my friend Judith. The man and I were having an affair. But despite the wrongness of it all, I was still excited about being a mother. The baby's father wanted me to go to Houston and have an abortion, but I refused. I was prepared to deal with all the consequences, just to have the chance to love that baby. I just knew that somehow, by being

157

a good, loving mother, I would erase the hurt, the hell that my own mother had inflicted upon me.

"Well, I kept the pregnancy hidden from family, especially from my mother. Then one night, I had a terrible nightmare. In the dream, I was lying on my mother's bed, just as I had that day I started my period. I could feel a hateful pain in my stomach and suddenly I was empty. I felt the most lonely, sorrowful emptiness I had ever felt in my life and there was my mother, standing there holding that black hair brush. And impaled on the end of the hair brush was my baby, now dead. She had ripped it from my womb.

"When I awoke, I realized that I had been dreaming, and at first felt great relief. But then I felt real pain, real cramps in my stomach. I went to the bathroom and discovered that I was bleeding. I sat down on the toilet and a large clump of blood came out, and with it, my baby. I woke Judith up, and she drove me to the emergency room at the Martin Parish hospital, where the attending physician informed me that I had indeed miscarried.

"She did it, I know she did. Somehow, in some way, my mother had managed to steal the one thing from me that would have made me happy. And I knew that day that I really wanted her dead."

The courtroom was once again as silent as a morgue as everyone listened to Bubbie's sorrowful story. I had had no idea that she had ever been pregnant and that made me even sadder as I imagined her going through that time all alone, without her family to support her.

Sorrowfully, wistfully, Richard said to the judge, "Nothing further, Your Honor."

"You may step down," Judge Holbrook said to Bubbie, a degree of sorrow in her voice as well.

With a startling bang of her gavel, the honorable Judge Holbrook recessed the court for the day. The next session would include final arguments and the fateful final address to the jury by both the defense and the prosecution. Bubbie was led away, and the rest of us began to file out of the courtroom. I met Richard out in the lobby.

"Sam, I had no idea about the diary. I don't know how they got it, but it really doesn't matter. Bubbie admits to killing your mother, it's just a matter of making the jury feel that she did it in much-delayed self defense, and not in cold blood. I am still confident that the jury will buy off on the Post Traumatic Stress Disorder angle, Sam."

"I hope so, Richard," I said. "I can't imagine Bubbie in prison."

"The final part of this trial will be on Tuesday of next week. For better or worse, it will be over," Richard said.

"You didn't call any more of my brothers or sisters to the stand. Any particular reason?" I asked, lighting a cigarette.

"I felt as though we had sufficiently established a pattern of abuse, Sammy," Richard said. "I just didn't see the need."

"Well, I'm grateful," I said, drawing deeply on the cigarette. "I'll be glad when this is finished, whatever the outcome."

"Try to have a good weekend, Sammy," Richard said.

"You too," I said, shaking Richard's hand.

Chapter 12

During that weekend, I found myself restless and anxious about the outcome of Bubbie's trial. But that wasn't the only reason for the restlessness. I pondered the events that had taken place since my return to Louisiana, and I had trouble putting it all into perspective. What if I had not come home for Rick's funeral? Would things have happened differently? Maybe Bubbie would not have killed Mama. Maybe none of this was really happening at all and I would wake up in my safe London flat, ready to have a cup of Earl Gray on the lanai. On Sunday, I went into Prescilla's bedroom for the first time since that fateful day when Bubbie had ended our mother's life.

The same chest of drawers that Bubbie had spoken about during her trial was still there, a hodgepodge of items taking up space on the top.

There was a photograph of my mother and father that had been taken when they had been young. Prescilla had been beautiful, and my father handsome. They looked like any other young couple, the newness of love brightening their faces. Had God known then, how tragic this young couple's life would turn out to be? I mean, God knows everything, right? And since He had known, why hadn't He done something to make things better?

I looked slowly around the room and my eyes fell on the bed; the very bed where Bubbie had been viciously attacked by our very cruel and very sick mother. A shudder shook my body as though a cold wind had passed through my very bones. Yes, there were ghosts there. They were present in the odds and ends of life that lay about the room. They were present in the furniture and in the walls and in the very soul of this damnable house.

Present in this place were the ghosts of our former selves. Nine children, who had long since ceased to be children, but had become complex troubled adults. As long as this house stood, those ghosts would continue to ramble about, rattling the chains of their lost innocence in the night. I wondered if they were aware of one another, as they moment by moment relived the terrible events that had trapped them there within the house's weather beaten wooden frame? They were indeed all there. The ghosts of our childhoods, divorced from the rational world, unable to escape their gloomy nonexistence.

My ghost would be in the bedroom down the hall, eternally leafing through a tattered issue of a National Geographic magazine, believing that he will never have the opportunity to visit any of the exotic, magical worlds depicted in the glossy photographs. Or perhaps he would be found swinging wildly through the air on the old rope swing down by the bayou, imagining that he would someday release his grip on the rope and fly away, soaring into the blue sky to land on some distant shore where his true father and mother awaited him.

And there in our mother's bedroom, the ghost of a little girl stood next to the bed, squinting against the bright shafts of sunlight that filtered into the room between the slats of the blinds. Within the faerie-motes of dust that only become visible in such shafts of light, the ghost simply stood, waiting for someone, *anyone* to see her there, a bloody wad of paper in her hand, a white bow in her beautiful black hair.

Throughout the cursed house, each of the little ghosts suffered in private. When would they be free, these little wraiths of the past? Standing there in the half-lit room, I realized that I was weeping.

Before I left the room, I looked around the sad space one final time. It was then that I realized that an additional ghost, which should have been there, was nowhere to be seen. I expected to see her in the yellowed strand of pearls on her dresser, or in the hairbrush on the bedside table. In fact, I tried to summon this inexplicably absent ghost, but to no avail. No, the ghost of our mother was not there. At first, I found it strange that I could not feel the residue of Prescilla's life in the house. Maybe Bubbie's chilling announcement of "it's over" was true. If so, then there no longer existed any power strong enough to bind the little ghosts to the house, except maybe the house itself. At that moment, I understood what had to be done to free them, and I made it my goal to see that it happened.

Tuesday morning found the Preston kids in the courtroom of the Martin Parish Covrt Hovse, waiting for the closing statements of both the defense and prosecution. We were all exhausted by that point, and the strain of the previous weeks was evident in our silence and utter lack of enthusiasm.

Richard was first to address the jury. At first, he just stood there, looking first at Bubbie, and then at us, and then at the jurors. I was beginning to think Richard was drunk or something, when he began to speak.

"I remember my favorite time of the day during my childhood," Richard began, pacing to and fro in front of the jury box. "It was three-thirty in the afternoon, every day. That was my favorite time of every day. You know why? Three-thirty in the afternoon was my favorite time of the day because it was at that specific time, when I was a child that I got off the school bus at my house and walked through the back door into the kitchen. Without fail, Gilligan's Island could be heard coming from the television in the den.

"Also without fail, my mother would be in the kitchen, pouring milk into a glass and setting it on the kitchen counter next to a walnut brownie. She would kiss my forehead and ask me how my day at school had been. It was a time of security. It was a time when, no matter what had happened at school, in the playground, or anywhere else, I knew that I was completely safe. Ladies and gentlemen of the jury, think for a moment, if you will indulge me, about your favorite time of day. Maybe it was like mine, that time when you got home from school. Maybe it was when supper was ready and you sat down to eat. Maybe it was a Sunday dinner when your grandparents and aunts and uncles came over. Whatever the case, ladies and gentlemen, these favorite times of the day have one thing in common: home; the feeling of being at home, with your mother or father. The feeling of security, when you were in your own element, when you were in a place where the bully from school, the mean teacher, the person who said hurtful things to you, when none of these things could touch you because you were at home with your mom or dad, or aunt or uncle - you felt safe. Are you there yet, ladies and gentlemen? Are you in that place? Maybe you are, maybe you aren't. Maybe you aren't because, like Miss Preston and her siblings, no such place exists for you. In fact, maybe you felt security when you were leaving the place where you lived. Maybe you understand what it was like for this family, to be beaten and struck down at every turn by the one person who was supposed to be your defender, your knight in shining armor, your hero? In the previous weeks, my dear jurors, you have heard the testimonies of each of these hurting people. You have heard firsthand what it was like to live in the same house with a sick and demented individual.

"Could you feel the spittle on your face, as Sam's mother spit on him? Could you feel the bits of glass rip into your flesh, as Miss Preston's mother bashed Miss Preston's head into the glass? Maybe you could feel the scratch of a brillo pad against your face as Ruth's mother scoured the makeup from Ruth's tender flesh."

Richard paused for a moment. Then he began to speak again. "Could you feel the handle of the brush...?" He abruptly stopped and just stared at the jurors. Some of them, especially the women in the jury, averted their eyes, or bowed their heads. Richard continued the emotional onslaught.

"Think for a moment what it must have been like to live with this particularly cruel type of abuse on a daily basis! For years -" Richard's voice began to rise in volume, passion evident in his words.

"For years they endured it. And to make it worse, they endured it while an entire community — *your community* - stood idly by and did absolutely *nothing* as it happened. And do you think the hurt just went away when these people finally, mercifully, grew old enough to escape the torment? Do the emotional scars just magically disappear? I think you know that they indeed do not go away that easily, and a person might spend her entire life trying to expunge herself of those things. Consider just for a moment, my dear jurors, that you were living these nightmares yourself and that after escaping, you suddenly found yourself faced with them again, years later. You heard the testimony of Professor Parkson. Average people, like you, when faced with a threat to life, will react to defend themselves from a perceived threat. This is precisely what transpired in this case that has been presented to you. Ladies and gentlemen, the woman you see before you, Iris Preston, did not kill her mother! It was Bubbie Preston, an abused, frightened little girl, who was simply acting to defend her own life. And likewise, if we, through a gross miscarriage of justice, decide to put this woman into prison, it won't be Iris Preston who is locked away. It will be Bubbie Preston, that same little girl who lived in dread fear from day to day. I am begging you, ladies and gentlemen, to please see that justice is carried out. This woman is no killer. And she doesn't belong in a prison with real criminals."

With one last pleading look, Richard returned to his seat. I must say that I was very impressed with Richard that day. For the first time I saw him as the successful adult that he was, and not the snot-nosed kid who had been my best friend in high school. His closing statements were awesome. Surely the jury would see it his way.

Next, the prosecution had a chance to address the jury and Mr. Dallas Guilbeau, the District Attorney, waddled his way to the jury box.

"Justice," he began. "My colleague just spoke about justice. Let's ask Prescilla Preston what she thinks about justice. Wait, we can't can we? We can't ask Prescilla Preston anything because she is dead, her life ended by the direct, cold-blooded actions of the monster sitting before you, Iris Preston. And yet the defense would have you believe, ladies and gentlemen, that the real monster -- was the victim! An old lady, a diminutive little old gray-haired lady, slain by one whom she should have been able to trust. Self defense? Defense from what? The defense would also have you believe that it was somehow okay for Iris Preston to murder her mother, because of some unproven, undocumented alleged abuse that Iris Preston claims took place almost thirty years ago! No, no ladies and gentlemen, this was clearly not a case of self defense. Iris Preston had been planning, for years apparently from what she wrote in her own diary, to murder her mother when the opportunity availed itself. And that is exactly what she did.

She took advantage of a sickly old woman. A sickly old woman, who was actually in the throes of mourning because of the death of her son! Oh dear jurors, I am thankful that you are a people of reason and that you will not allow yourselves to be sucked into this strange psychosis shared by Iris Preston and her siblings.

"There is only one possible outcome to this trial that will ensure that justice is done. I trust that you, the jury, with objectivity and reason, will return a verdict of guilty in this case. Iris Preston belongs in prison, where she will never be allowed to murder again."

Okay, I thought, this guy is good, too. When Dallas Guilbeau finished his remarks, I had a sinking feeling that replaced the exultation I had felt when Richard had finished his own remarks. It was all up to the jury now. I really didn't know what to expect as I watched the jury file out of the chamber do deliberate my sister's fate.

To everyone's surprise, it only took about thirty minutes for them to reach a verdict. I looked over at Richard and he mouthed the words, "it's a good thing," referring to the short deliberation time. Soon the jurors were once again seated. Judge Holbrook addressed the Jury Foreman. "Has the jury reached a verdict?" she asked.

"Yes, Your Honor," the foreman replied.

"How say you?"

"Your Honor, in the case of the People of the State of Louisiana versus Miss Iris Preston, on the charge of murder in the second degree, we the jury find the defendant Iris Preston -- guilty."

Nobody, I mean nobody in that courtroom, including myself or the most honorable Sandra Holbrook expected this verdict. A rumble filled the courtroom and Judge Holbrook had to bang her gavel several times to restore order. I listened in disbelief as the judge asked each individual juror, "how say you," and each time the response was "guilty."

I was dumbfounded, as were my brothers and sisters, and Richard Romero as well. The only person in the room who didn't seem to be upset about the verdict was Bubbie. She exuded that same sense of serenity that I had seen in her when the trial had first begun. For some reason, her calm acceptance of the verdict infuriated me, and I lost control. I stood up and faced the jury box.

"I bet you all beat your kids, you fucking assholes," I yelled toward the jury. "Fuck each and every one of you," I continued as an angry Judge Holbrook inanely banged her gavel. "You've just said to the world, loudly and clearly, that people can abuse their children with impunity, don't you fucking idiots see that?" I was still yelling as two officers drug me from the courtroom.

Everyone was to be back inside the loathsome courtroom one more time, and that would be for sentencing on the next day. Everyone that is, except me. I was ticketed for causing a public disturbance and banned from the rest of the proceedings. It was a good decision, because I probably would have lost control again.

The following day, I stayed at the old house and waited for Denise to call me to relate Bubbie's sentence. It was okay with me, because a day alone at the house gave me a chance to prepare for what would take place later that evening, when my siblings all came out to the Preston place one last time.

My cell phone rang at about eleven-thirty that morning. It was Denise. Bubbie had been sentenced to seven years in the Louisiana Correctional Institute for Women in Baton Rouge. Denise said that Judge Holbrook actually seemed remorseful about giving Bubbie the sentence. Denise also said that Bubbie seemed irrationally happy during the sentencing. I pondered this for a moment and decided that no, it was not irrational for Bubbie to have such a degree of happiness. The difference between being free and being bound was defined in much different terms for Bubbie than for an average person. Although made to stay inside a cinderblock building, without the option leave, Bubbie was freer inside those walls than she had ever been on the outside. She was finally free from the phantoms that had haunted her for so long. But most importantly, she was finally free from Prescilla Preston.

Chapter 13

B y the time my brothers and sisters arrived out at the old house, I had everything ready. It really hadn't been all that difficult to prepare. No one had really wanted to keep anything from inside the old house. While I had been waiting, I had lit a small bon fire down by the gazebo. I was standing by the fire, poking the burning logs with a long stick when everyone showed up. One by one my brothers and sisters joined me by the fire.

"I guess you'll return to London," Ruth said, putting her arm around me.

"Yeah," I answered. "My life is really there now. But I promise I will come back to visit at least once or twice a year."

"What about ya'll?" I asked to everyone else. Faye spoke up.

"Well, we'll just go back to our lives, I guess," she said, sighing deeply. "I have grandchildren to think about.

We'll go visit Bubbie on visitation days and just wait for her to be released. Richard said she was getting "good time" whatever that is, and could actually be released before the seven years is up."

"I'll keep working as a nurse," Ruth said. "I only have a few more years to work until I'm eligible to retire."

"What about you, Trevor," I asked, moving closer to my eldest brother.

"Well, Sammy, there are still people who need to hear the gospel, so I'll have to go back to the camp," he answered. I simply nodded my head in agreement.

Brett spoke up.

"I'm moving to Texas," he said. No one was surprised. "I'm going to work for a construction company in Waco."

"Well I'm staying right where I am," Renee said. "In a couple of years, my children will graduate, and then, I don't know, maybe Rob and I will get that cabin in Colorado we've always dreamed about."

In unison, everyone turned to look at Rand. Without Rick, Rand would be completely lost, and we all knew it.

"What?" Rand barked, feigning irritation. "Why's everyone staring at me?" Faye giggled first, and soon everyone was laughing, enjoying a needed emotional lift.

"Cora has always wanted a little house on Toledo Bend Lake," Rand said. "It was Rick's favorite place to go camping and fishing. I imagine we will be living up there by the end of the year."

For the next several moments everyone just stood there, poking in the fire and looking around the place for what would be the last time. Quietly I walked to the gazebo and retrieved the seven wooden sticks I had prepared earlier that day. I had wrapped the ends of the sticks with scraps from some old bath towels and soaked them in diesel. Without offering any explanation, I handed each of my brothers and sisters a stick. No explanation was needed. Each person understood exactly what we were going to do. We gathered around the fire and each of us placed the ends of our sticks into the flames, igniting the wads of cloth.

In silence we walked slowly but purposefully toward the old clapboard house. The ailing structure seemed to sense what was coming. The roofline seemed to sag more than usual and the window sashes drooped like the eyes of a criminal who has just resigned himself to the fact the he is about to be executed. I was the first to touch my torch to the peeling clapboard. I was surprised at how quickly the wood caught fire. One by one my brothers and sisters touched their torches to the house, until the entire east side was aflame.

No one spoke as we retreated to the area around the gazebo to stand still and watch as the hungry flames quickly spread to the rest of the house. As eager as I had been to see the place gone, a brief pain, perhaps sparked by a sudden burst of nostalgia, stabbed my heart. Just before the house completely disappeared inside the flames, I watched as the blooms on the Camp Jasmine that grew outside Mama's window first wilted, then caught fire, then turned to ash.

Chapter 14

The sky had been beautiful the night we set fire to the old house. The millions of embers that emanated from the conflagration created a magnificent display against the velvet backdrop of night, its beauty competing with that of the shimmering stars. The Preston kids stood there together and watched and listened as the house plunged into the throes of its death. The rafters moaned and then fell, the roof caving in upon the rest of the house.

Everyone remained silent as we watched the spectacle. Suddenly, my eyes were drawn to side of the house, where an old cracked concrete sidewalk led from what was left of the house to the driveway. I rubbed my eyes, thinking that the smoke was making me see things, but no, the image was still there. Standing in the driveway, barely perceptible but there nonetheless, was a group of children. They were holding hands and seemed to be dancing around in a circle. Yes, they were *dancing*. Each child wore a broad smile as they circled and circled to music that only they could hear. Suddenly the circle opened and the children began to dance in a line. On one end, a tiny child with a look of glee on his tender face struggled to keep up with the rest of the children. It was then that I saw, in what had been the center of the circle, a little girl wearing shiny new shoes and a white bow in her beautiful black hair. She ran to the end of the line and took the hand of the tiny child who was having trouble keeping up. Joviality written upon each countenance the children danced down the driveway, their images becoming more and more difficult to make out. And then, just before they winked out of sight, the little girl wearing the shiny new shoes and the white bow in her beautiful black hair paused for a moment, smiled at me, and disappeared.

S.M. Bankman
28 January 2006
Carville, Louisiana

Breinigsville, PA USA
07 July 2010
241348BV00001B/17/P

9 781432 749583